the americas

ADVISORY BOARD

Irene Vilar, series editor

Edna Acosta-Belén
Daniel Alarcón
Frederick Luis Aldama
Esther Allen
Homero Aridjis
Harold Augenbraum
Stanley H. Barkan
Junot Díaz
Dedi Felman
Rosario Ferré
Jean Franco
Rigoberto González
Edith Grossman
Naomi Lindstrom
Adriana V. López

Jaime Manrique
Mirta Ojito
Gavin O'Toole
Bud Parr
Margaret Sayers Peden
Gregory Rabassa
Luis J. Rodriguez
Lissette Rolón-Collazo
Rossana Rosado
Bob Shacochis
Daniel Shapiro
Mónica de la Torre
Silvio Torres-Saillant
Doug Unger
Oscar Villalon

Daughter of Silence

Manuela Fingueret

Translated by Darrell B. Lockhart

Texas Tech University Press

Copyright © 2012 by Manuela Fingueret; translation copyright © 2012 Darrell B. Lockhart.

Originally published as *Hija del silencio*, copyright © 1999 by Manuela Fingueret.

Work published within the framework of "SUR" Translation Support Program of the Ministry of Foreign Affairs, International Trade and Worship of the Argentine Republic.
The publisher and author appreciate the financial support for translation of *Daughter of Silence*.

All rights reserved. No portion of this book may be reproduced in any form or by any means, including electronic storage and retrieval systems, except by explicit prior written permission of the publisher. Brief passages excerpted for review and critical purposes are excepted.

This book is typeset in Fairfield. The paper used in this book meets the minimum requirements of ANSI/NISO Z39.48–1992 (R1997). [infinity]

Designed by Kasey McBeath

Library of Congress Cataloging-in-Publication Data
Fingueret, Manuela.
    [Hija del silencio. English]
    Daughter of silence / Manuela Fingueret ; translated by Darrell B. Lockhart.
        p. cm. — (The Americas)
    Summary: "A novel intertwining the voices of a mother and her daughter—women shaped and separated by violent historical moments—revealing unspoken parallels between the Holocaust and Argentina's 'Dirty War'"—Provided by publisher.
    ISBN 978-0-89672-731-1 (pbk. : alk. paper)
    I. Lockhart, Darrell B. II. Title.
    PQ7798.16.I54H5513 2012
    863'.64—dc23   2011051768

Printed in the United States of America
12 13 14 15 16 17 18 19 20 / 9 8 7 6 5 4 3 2 1

Texas Tech University Press
Box 41037 | Lubbock, Texas 79409-1037 USA
800.832.4042 | ttup@ttu.edu | www.ttupress.org

To our generation, sons and daughters of
the Shoah and survivors of the
Argentine military dictatorship (1976–1982).

To the Fundación Memoria del Holocausto
(Buenos Aires, Argentina).

I share this novel with those who, in one way or another,
helped me to accurately research circumstances and facts.

To Erika Blumgrund and Jack Fuchs,
who courageously and creatively endured.

Introduction

Manuela Fingueret, a native of Buenos Aires, is one of Argentina's foremost contemporary authors and a leading intellectual figure. Early in her career she earned a considerable reputation as a poet. Her first novel, *Blues de la calle Leiva* (Leiva Street Blues, 1995) clearly demonstrated her talent as a novelist. To date she has published three novels, all of which have garnered critical acclaim. *Daughter of Silence* is her second novel, originally published in Spanish in 1999 as *Hija del silencio*. In general, Fingueret's literature is born out of her experience and her identity as an Argentine Jew, an identity she embraces and views as being culturally complex and dually enriching.

Argentina is home to the largest Jewish population in Latin America and one of the largest in the world (figures vary as to what place Argentina occupies in this regard). While the story of Jewish immigration to Argentina primarily has been marked by success and triumph over adversity, it has not been without its troubled moments. Fingueret's novel is the first and one of only a very few literary works to link the experience of the Shoah to Argentina's neofascist military dictatorship, given the euphemistic appellation of "Process of National Reorganization" (1976–1983). The novel's uniquely Jewish perspective draws painful parallels between Argentina's military *Proceso* and the Holocaust, separated by time and geography but united in their brutality, inhumanity, and the suffering they created.

Fingueret weaves a cautionary tale from the stories of two women, mother and daughter, who are detached by silence yet bound together by history. The stories of daughter Rita, a young Jewish political prisoner in Argentina, and that of her mother Tinkeleh, a Holocaust survivor, are alternately narrated as they collide in the fragmented memory of Rita. Resistance and survival are common themes in the lives of the two women. Tortured, starved, and locked up in a dank, barren prison cell Rita struggles to maintain her sense of reality and of self. As a survival technique she probes the depths of her memory to reconstruct her own past as well as that of her mother. Through undergoing much of the same suffering as her mother underwent she begins to understand her mother's silence and emotional distance, and ultimately to come to terms with the nature of the relationship with her mother.

Rita's story is disjointed, told in incomplete sentences, and filled with fleeting images that are seemingly disconnected. It was particularly challenging to translate her narrative voice into English and maintain the same fragmentary expression—a consequence of her circumstance and psychological frailty—in a way that conveys the emotional authenticity of the original. Gaps, missing information, and above all silence permeate the novel such that translation became an exercise in communicating what is absent from the written text. The stories of Rita and Tinkeleh are constructed around a series of voids across time and geographical boundaries. They are stories—both individual and universal—that are too often repeated and which should never be forgotten.

Darrell B. Lockhart

Daughter of Silence

When Evita Perón entered into immortality, for the first time I became acutely aware of the relationship between things that demand our undivided attention and daily life, which only pretends to go on around us.

Since then, winter has always smelled of death to me. The perfume of jasmine announcing the arrival of summer, butterflies, hair and clothing flowing in the breeze, allowed me to imagine I could find a new place in my world. I seemed to drag the rest around with me like a burden, an unsettling awareness of shapeless spaces created by my mother and set adrift on a ship that never fully set anchor in the port of Buenos Aires. With time I became the captain of that ghost ship. Her attempts to conceal that legacy were brimming with food, layers of warm clothing and, at times a gentle embrace during my weekly bath that she gave to me in the tub filled with warm water. A longing caress, warm, snug, moist, felt through the towel.

"Essay topic": Mother's Day. I used to invent a different Tinkeleh for this homework assignment. She opened my notebook once, which almost never happened, and came across the image of her own unrecognizable face. She didn't know what to say. She would have loved to say something, but breaking the pact of silence between us was unthinkable. Her heavy sigh became the strongest element of the bond between us.

My father is a meticulous storyteller, from Bible stories to family chronicles. I learned from him to follow the paths of exotic tales that took place both in the realm of fantasy and the concrete world. We covered it all, from using tools or making adhesive to fix furniture, to delving into the Jewish past through literature and interweaving the stories of ancestors and those close to us. How we cherished those moments together.

In school there were three basic subject areas: letters, numbers, and useless things. I love letters, I detest numbers, and I was forced to take useless things. Cross-stitch, for example, mending old socks, sewing a hem on a skirt. I felt like dashing off to the worlds I discovered wide-eyed with my father. I preferred a hundred times over the macramé shoulder bags, the fishing rods, and the carving boards that the boys made to those insipid chores of "young ladies." The way social roles are assigned is appalling; pre-arranged attitudes and roles ruin the fun in everything.

She's here again, sustaining a windstorm of memories with *yerba mate* and milk. Here, in this place, she's stuck to my skin, tattooed like a number.

Hysterical teachers who yell more than they speak, neighborhood women whose words are as frayed as their bedroom slippers, all passing through life on the installment plan. That's how I felt at times, like I was on a payment plan, always choosing between woodworking and cross-stitch, or the bread that makes up the body and soul of Tinkeleh. Those that she cared and longed for remain hidden amongst the shadows. My world consisted of the afternoon soaps or the Cine Lux radio show on Saturday night. Fernando Siro and Rosa Rosen, Julio César Barton and "The Princess Who Wanted to Live." I imagined my own Gregory Peck getting out of his Fiat 600 to take me in his arms. And, of course, there were the books with which I created my living environment. Being able to discover the melody hidden behind words turned me into an avid reader, an attentive listener, and a subtle observer. Among the white pages and the silence, I was able to interpret the symbols of a narrative that transpires between what's known as reality and the afternoon soaps.

Smokes, *yerba mate*, literature. Saratoga, Cruz Malta, Corín Tellado. *Yerba mate*, smokes, literature. Taragüí, Le Mans, Simone de Beauvoir. Literature, *yerba mate,* and smokes. Emily Dickenson, Cruz Malta, and Marlboro. Choosing. An obsession? Or militancy? Tinkeleh, Rivka, Hannah, Eva Perón. Without repeating or stalling. *Mate*, literature, smokes, militancy. That's how it got started. In that order. Unsweetened *mate* with milk, lots of poetry, some novels, constant reading, filtered cigarettes, and a lot of smoke to fill my lungs with Evita.

My father played the role of fire stoker in all this. Topics and concerns: the destiny of Israel, the survival of Judaism, chess, Yiddish, a few legendary writers. A narrative I've been embroidering since adolescence with a sloppy but convincing stitch. Every once in a while I completed a woodworking project that took the home economics teacher by surprise. That's how I made up for the embarrassment over the horrible scarf I knitted wider that it was long or the unacceptable knickers that turned out like briefs and made me the butt of jokes about my so-called feminine abilities.

At fifteen I added splendid tales about heroes and novels with various Quixotes. I invented stories while daydreaming of her and watching her slowly drift off. I also included the Zionist fervor of my father, who considered himself a reservist at the ready to be called upon by the Israeli army. I left aside the neighborhood girls, so close and yet so far from being the women that I desired them to be and that they refused to be. Goodbye, Glostora Tango Club, Cine Lux Radio, Samson and Delilah, forever. I crumpled them all into a ball and I threw it into a little container I used for a wastebasket. We shall meet again in one of Che Guevara's chapters, in Neruda's "Heights of Machu Picchu," or in the punches thrown by Bonavena. With or without them, within reach of Roberto Arlt or one of his melancholy ruffians who take me in along the way and we keep each other company without making any demands.

No demands? Those were the days! I, who molded myself in the image and likeness of duty.

A hand claws at this hood underneath which I desperately try to breathe. What else will they do if I don't play by the rules? Do they have any concept of mercy? What are you rambling about, Rita? Am I who I hoped to be or am I the hand that pulls at this rag as if it were the curtain for a show that demands many encores? I'm an actress in an unstable cast of characters. I'm a momentary detour in her sea of uncertainty. I did set anchor in the Río de la Plata, and in this unrecognizable frozen morgue that's overflowing with viscous anger-filled bodies, in a fierce struggle with that hell they try to reproduce in their harsh cackles.

Tinkeleh, Rivka, Hannah, Evita. Am I headed in your direction? Toward each one of you? Life flows from them into me. The furtive passion of what I desired, of what I don't yet know, of all they inspired in me flows from me to them.

I drag them with me as I drag myself desperately along.

Tinkeleh found me both entertaining and unmanageable, which frightened her and made her proud at the same time. When I got into trouble, she would chase after me with an old shoe. She could never catch me and I'd hear her threats in the distance as I fled to safety. She was capable of unleashing incredible fury. Then, when Papa came home from work I would return under his protection, holding his hand and with a smile of victory on my face. At that moment she hated us both, and it made me feel like the heroine in one of the Bible stories he used to tell me.

When I'd catch her lost in thought, I would sit next to her in silence. She would go off to some unreachable place while she hummed a tune learned from her mother: *Liulinke main meidele, Liulinke main kind/ . . .*

That's how her name Tinkeleh ("Blackie") acquired the intensity of a shared return, a strange mixture of affection and distance at the same time. In silence we longed for places that had once belonged to her. A secret pact that—I didn't yet know—would unite us forever.

I discovered that very possibility several years later in the thinking of Che Guevara and in the passion of Eva Perón. Evita, who died one winter evening at 8:25 p.m., was reborn in me with the fury of woman who wasn't allowed to fulfill her destiny. Che

Guevara gave both of us reason and strength. With the two of them I carved the framework of a destiny that turned me into Lot's wife, she who dared to gaze at what was hidden from her. She was nameless, but courageous. But I, who planned to stare directly at Sodom and Gomorrah, had no intention of being turned into a pillar of salt.

The silence wields needles capable of piercing anything, even this wall, a shapeless mass that I manage to make out for the first time. How long has it been? Days? Weeks? I've lost all sense of orientation. I cannot feel my body. An acrid odor is the only thing I can distinguish clearly. I have the images of faces stuck in my throat and an undulating wound circulates through my body like a lonely worm. *Tenia Saginata*, Miss, my zoology teacher would have told me. *Tenia Saginata* is the nausea that creeps along at a 2/4 beat. Alfredo de Angelis. An appropriate rhythm for the occasion. What does that have to do with anything now? I smile at my silly free association and I'm relieved.

I move slowly toward her lap. It's an autumn afternoon and she's seated nearby picking the nits off me. The silence is overwhelming in this unfathomable steppe that surrounds us. I'd like to have had that old shopkeeper's notepad with black oilskin covers in which I jotted down notes or some verse that seemed to foretell a future poem: "Flowers don't puff up with pride, they only briefly resist time," I wrote. An expression of Tinkeleh's: "*Got alein veist!*" That "Only God knows!" that she repeated like a litany when faced with the unforeseen, which I sketched into a drawing on one of the pages. Numerous short prayers like the plumes of smoky silence that she left smoldering within me.

Eduardo Galeano's phrases from *The Open Veins of Latin America* and the Peronism of Eva resounding in the pages of *The Reason for My Life*. My usual afternoon soap, but with a passion replete with symbols that I took great pains to decipher.

I felt that my Eva was her, my Tinkeleh, the Tinkeleh who at one time had traveled across Europe where she had remained forever. I could be her return.

The black oilskin notepad contained the expressions of women who moved me with their attitudes, actions, and words. Returning to them helps me to remember who I was, like Haydée with whom I didn't learn dressmaking, but who showed me how to live in a different skin than the one that they're trying to scorch today. Woman and women braided together like cords of macramé or stuck together with wood glue into a single piece needing patient sanding and polishing.

Woman and women. Either from the old neighborhood or uptown. All of them, whether from Minsk, the Chacarita neighborhood, or dancing the anniversary waltz around the Obelisk in downtown Buenos Aires. They are with me in this animal cage, registered by first and last name, smiling like hyenas with each jolt of electricity.

Among them is Haydée who swings her hips to her own beat. She leads me out onto the street and signals me to follow her.

Haydée was the daughter of Juan Carlos Appe, a mattress maker. Since childhood she stood out from her siblings because of her languid, opaque stare. Juanita, the oldest sister, married young and pregnant; Olga, the youngest girl, had little ambition and imitated her in every way; Juan and Jorge, her brothers, businessmen from a very young age. I remember them making small boats out of nutshells or dollhouses of different sizes out of Tomasito string boxes that they painted and sold to unwilling customers.

Haydée and Olga played with Jorge, the better looking of the two brothers, as if he were a doll. They dressed him in skirts, styled his shiny blond hair in curls, and painted his thick lips scarlet red. Part of the game was for the three of them to climb under the sheets in their father's bed. It was during those games that both Haydée and Olga discovered the pleasure of the forbidden.

When Haydée turned twelve years old, their father died. She scarcely even noticed his absence. She rarely saw him since he left early in morning and returned at night. On Sundays he would greet them coarsely, his clothes covered in wool lint and several days' worth of growth in his beard. He'd force himself to eat some soup and then go lie down for a nap. Haydée's mother spent her afternoons in meetings at Sara's shop, or chasing after her kids with a shoe when they brought bad grades home from school. Haydée had no interest in studying. When she finished the sixth grade and her mother suggested she learn dressmaking at the academy on the corner of Seguí and San Martín Avenue, she accepted unenthusiastically. It was all the same to her if she learned to sew or style hair. Her mother, who did freelance sewing work for some Jews in the Once neighborhood, hoped to share that skill with Haydée.

Meanwhile, much against her will Olga began training at the Business School. In reality, she wanted to go with her sister to the Dressmaking Academy, but their mother was against it because she had dreamed of her daughter becoming an office worker who could rub elbows with the downtown crowd. She didn't want Olga to have the same fate as Juanita, and she had little confidence in Haydée's future.

We met at the bus stop. Haydée rode home on Tuesdays and Thursdays from the sewing school and I from typing classes at the Pitman School on San Martín Avenue and Donato Álvarez.

In the beginning neither of us took much notice of the other. After a few days we glanced at each other out of the corners of our eyes, and then we began to say hello to one another, until one day Haydée invited me for a bite to eat at the pizzeria that was just down the street from the academy. I hesitated at first, but eventually accepted since I was drawn to that type of personality, especially if they appeared suddenly, as if thrust onto the scene by something that I imagined was arranged from another galaxy.

Haydée's words poured out in gushes, but without any trace of inflection in her voice. She told me about her siblings and about Warnes Street, where she lived; about the dark apartment on the first floor, of her longing to travel to far off places and meet interesting people. She spoke without periods or commas, like the actress Niní Marshall's character La Catita. I liked her.

It was strange that a girl her age showed no enthusiasm for anything, except when it came to men. Then her blank eyes took on an unusual expression, a kind of fiery sensuality that made her fascinating.

I listened to her with great interest, but also with a condescending stare that replaced the superiority I once felt over the other inhabitants of the neighborhood. I was drawn to them, but at the same time their mediocrity infuriated me. I inherited that disdain for the ignorance of others from my father, who considered uncultured people to be willing pariahs. To him they were schmucks, or imbeciles, and he often repeated that "they're only alive because the air they breathe is free."

I smile to think what he would say if he were to see me sitting there with Haydée, listening to her stories about brothers and sisters and the games played beneath the sheets in the one bedroom they all shared.

She spoke of things in which I hadn't yet dared to delve. I was just starting down a path toward a world gone crazy, and I was determined to make it my duty to change it. In that upside down world, sex was a disruptive element, though I must admit, I found it enthralling and provocative at the same time. For me life was a synthesis between Simone de Beauvoir and Eva Perón. Yes, I analyzed everything. I analyze everything. I analyze myself, I describe and I pronounce. I speak, then I act. I think, then I act. I think and speak, then I act.

That was my analysis of Haydée. Nevertheless, I couldn't ignore the feelings that she stimulated in my body. The disdain I felt in the beginning turned into a twinge of envy, a humiliating feeling but nonetheless troubling when I had to witness the tremendous display of pleasure that she showed for certain things.

One day Haydée said we weren't going to eat pizza because she wanted to show me a special place, beneath the bridge on San Martín Avenue. I followed her.

We were standing on the corner when Haydée pointed to a house with a large green wooden door.

"See that," she told me. "That's a whorehouse."

My heart beat wildly as Haydée described, in her usual monotonous but candid way, things that they had told her about, things which were completely foreign to me because up until then I didn't know anything about the life that went on parallel to that of my heroines.

We ran frantically for the bus stop. Haydée kept looking at me every so often and smiling mischievously. Some boys on the bus staring directly at Haydée's pointy breasts created a strange mixture of anxiety and suffocation that caused me to squeeze my legs together with ferocity and pleasure. To this day both God and the Devil keep struggling for a place in my head.

I skipped typing class on Thursday. I didn't go to the next class either. When I went back, two weeks later, I ran anxiously to the bus stop but Haydée wasn't there. I wanted to ask her about things I'd been wrestling with during the days and nights I was unable to sleep, with my hand between my thighs, sweaty and ecstatic under the sheets. I had let two buses go by when finally I saw her coming down the sidewalk.

She was wearing a skirt she'd made in her class. It was white poplin with two slits up the sides that provided a glimpse of her white, slightly chubby yet shapely legs. She was also wearing the red banlon top her brother Juancito had given to her, all the rage that season. Her firm breasts and provocative nipples filled the Virtus bra that was specially made for busty girls who liked to show it off. She wore a red band in her hair and her carmine-painted lips caught the attention of men and women alike.

"Are you coming with me under the bridge?" she asked as if in passing.

"I can't," I answered, forgetting all the questions that I had hoped to ask her. I lowered my head, embarrassed by my own cowardice. Haydée shot me a look of indifference and left me there alone and speechless at the bus stop.

I didn't go back to typing class. I told my mother I would re-take it sometime down the road. That the professor was no good.

Years passed. Haydée was no longer among my concerns, until that afternoon when I was walking down Corrientes Avenue between Talcahuano and Callao, popping into as many bookstores as I could. Coming across her face in the heart of downtown was like opening a wound that never really had scarred over.

I recognized her immediately. Wrapped in tight-fitting brightly colored clothes, her hair dyed, the headband, her tits front and center. She was passing in front of La Giralda café.

My look of surprise made her react as if she'd seen a ghost and she hugged me letting out a little squeal of excitement. I invited her in to the bar for a cup of coffee. It was obvious that La Giralda was not Haydée's usual hangout. The yellowed marble and all the young people gathered around the tables were part of my world, but not hers. At first she seemed uncomfortable, but after a bit she launched right into conversation.

"What have you been up to?" I ventured, asking an intentionally open question.

"Same as always," Haydée answered flatly. "Same as always I help out my old lady. Juan got married and now works full-time upholstering foam rubber mattresses since few people use the stuffed ones anymore. Juanita has five kids, poor thing, and she works like madwoman. Olga's at the university studying to be an accountant. We all chip in to help her finish her degree. And Jorge, who studied to be a hair stylist, has a job at a dance club and he's engaged, poor thing."

"Why's he a poor thing?" I asked.

"Because he hooked up with the daughter of Cacerola Torres, and as soon as she finds out he's half queer, she'll beat him senseless."

Listening to her made me nervous.

"And you?" I said to her.

"I sew and screw," she muttered half laughing. "Listen, sweetie, the things life has to offer women are for my sisters, or for you. Since I'm no good at studying, I realized that I like tango halls, partying, and just enough work to buy myself some rags, a pizza, or take in a movie, which I still like to do as much as I did back then." She didn't make any references to the past and I didn't dare to either. "Well, girl, I'll leave you my number in case you want to give me a ring some time. Just one thing before I go, and don't be offended, but you seem a little stiff, a little 'tight-assed.' Sorry, but that's how you seem." Having said that she burst into laughter and called the waiter over to pay the bill.

I didn't let her pay: "This is my turf," I explained. Haydée thanked me, gave me a kiss on the cheek and shouted "Call me!" from the doorway.

I furiously tore up the scrap of paper with her phone number on it. Haydée is part of a world that I came close to once, a springboard into lives plagued by misunderstandings, which I gradually left behind when I abandoned the old neighborhood and traveled into the heart of the city without any stops along the way.

This dark damp wall is now a mirror. Memories provide a small measure of warmth that this place refuses to grant.

Haydée, a tiny piece of me with its own distinct weight. Haydée, your skin prickles, my skin condemns.

How I'd like to go back to that bus stop on San Martín Avenue!

Attempting to become a heroine, Tinkeleh's avenger, like some character in a novel or movie, was an exaggerated effort on my part. Maybe this choice was a fantasy, a leap toward the pillar of salt that I refused to be but that I kept feeding with impulsive fascination, a way to not keep quiet or to set myself apart from her, the woman from Mezeritch, from Minsk, from Terezin. From those others, the small-minded neighbor ladies played in the movies by actresses like Laura Hidalgo and Zully Moreno. And of coexisting with the heroines that nurtured my Judith as she attempted to overcome Holofernes.

Am I now paying for that distancing from myself with which I defined life?

They told me that no one can withstand torture for more than twelve hours, and yet they haven't been able to break me.

Am I Judith, or am I only pretending to be her?

I confuse everything. Did my mother act this way in order to survive? I ask in a hushed voice, but I am less sure of things now than then.

Then, what is then? Then is not long ago, it's yesterday. In here every hour encompasses all of time.

I can't even say if I would escape from Haydée like I did before. I also can't deny that I programmed an end; like this one? That terrifies me. It means destiny, and destiny is the excuse used by those who rule the world. My world cast in the image and likeness of destiny.

Program, destiny, struggle, grand words, and the opposite of Haydée. An Haydée whom I fled from in order to not be trapped in the old neighborhood, in its streets, in the typewriter, in the whorehouse on San Martín Avenue underneath the bridge.

4

Minsk, September 1941.

The city of Minsk is occupied and the streets are thick with tension. Tinkeleh enters Hanka's bakery.

"Any news today?" she asks under her breath, fearing the answer.

Hanka keeps her head lowered.

"You haven't heard anything new?" she insists.

She hears a heavy sigh.

"Did they take someone away?" she asks in a hushed voice.

Hanka finally raises her head to look at her. Tinkeleh's young age weighs heavily upon her. An enormous weight that she never felt before, when her small universe of streets and friends was unrestricted.

Hanka wraps her hot loaf of bread and places it in her hands. She looks at her again with a tenderness that Tinkeleh believes all bakers have. Baking bread always seemed to her to be the task of angels.

Tinkeleh breathes in the intense aroma of the bakery that filters through the white embroidered curtains. Curtains made of thin fabric that allows one to peek inside, catching just a glimpse. At the other bakery in town there's a greater variety of rye bread, but Hanka's bread lasts up to a week without drying out. Since flour is scarce, the bread loaves are continually smaller and less consistent. One can't even get bread on a daily basis, but they set some aside each week for her and her mother.

Tinkeleh sets off running with the warm loaf held tightly against her chest. She searches the empty streets for some familiar sign. She misses the bustling of the people in the market and the children playing among them.

She stumbles along as if the entire village were shaking beneath her feet. The bread warms her chest and her breath rattles within her. She needs to see Menachem.

She arrives home troubled, anxious; not even there does she feel safe.

The small room has everything the three of them need. They eat, read, write, and spend time talking together. She sleeps in a small loft reached by ladder. It's a tight space that accommodates a bed and her beloved possessions. Her reproductions of works by Cézanne and Turner hang on the wood paneled wall.

Her mother is seated on the wooden chair, watching the steam rise from the stewpot whose aroma floods the room. The slightly faded print dress and the dark-colored woven jacket give her worried face a hardened appearance. Tinkeleh notices that she looks tired. She sits down next to her on the wooden bench her father made and places the warm bread in her hands.

Hannah barely musters a smile for her daughter. She thinks to herself: "How she's grown these past few months!"

They have little patience for reading, so they tell each other stories about the town, sing old melodies that warm their hearts, or Hannah adds some Hasidic tale to the long repertoire she's been transmitting to her daughter.

"Did anyone arrive?" Hannah asks. "Did Hanka have any news to report?"

She wants to spare her more pain, so she answers with a question.

"And here, did any one come by?"

"Just Leah," she replies. "She brought some potatoes she got and in exchange I gave her some firewood. I'm so fortunate to have you to bring something from the woods or the bakery." Her mother suddenly stands up, takes the broom and sweeps the dust.

She hears her murmur: "Damned Russians! Damned Germans!"

Hannah has dark hair, dulled now by the dust that floats about the house, which she no longer bothers to minimize by wetting the broom in water liked she used to do.

They speak little to one another. Like two lionesses, they both protect and attack each other. However, they're more ready for a scrap than a caress. They sense that times are changing, but they are incapable of talking about it. At times she doesn't known if it's because they wish to protect one another or if they distrust the strength of the other.

Tinkeleh finds refuge in her loft. She has everything she needs there: paper, paintbrushes, colored pencils, a book or two she was unable to return to the school library on time, folders with drawings, reproductions.

She looks at the works by Leonardo Da Vinci, Rubens, and Velázquez in the book on painting that she'd received for her birthday. For her, the universe is made of form, color, light, and shadow. Her parents weren't pleased that she chose an activity that was not well viewed among Jews, but they didn't insist. She dedicates more time than ever to her painting. So as not to make her parents uncomfortable, she doesn't paint human images, leaning instead toward landscapes and still life in imitation of Cézanne to whom she was introduced by Leah. Leah comes from a nonreligious home with progressive beliefs that are too much for the Jews of this city, who look down on her parents and others who distance themselves from Orthodox Judaism. Nevertheless, Tinkeleh is amazed to discover that the majority of those young people who dress like gentiles are the first to speak out against the calamity that will befall the Jews who don't flee in time to Palestine or America. The Orthodox pray and passively await the destiny that God has in store for them. This riles her up because her parents vacillate between the two modes of thinking and she, by nature uncomfortable with generalizations, senses that those who are in contact with the outside world are better able to see the future.

Leah's parents also believe that the right choice is emigration, but with such a big family and no money it's difficult for them to make the move.

"Your family should leave, Tinkeleh," they tell her, "Later on it will be too late."

She agrees, though she can't imagine ever leaving Minsk. Why? Because of some crazed lunatic? Because of a bunch of lunatics? She ponders the question, like Leah's father, with an indignant look on her face.

Her own father, however, would be willing to try. She knows it. But her mother, Hannah, comes from a religious, Orthodox family, full of prejudices and fears. Marriage to her father had been a challenge and a family disgrace that cost her dearly. For Hannah abandoning Minsk would be another unbearable uprooting.

The summer flew by bringing vague news reports, anxiety, and undesirable prospects for the future.

5

Minsk, October 1941.

Winter is on the way, but it's not just the cold that keeps people off the town streets. Tinkeleh sometimes looks for discreet places where she can meet up with Menachem. They don't speak much, but they share books, which help them to keep going in the face of what they don't entirely understand.

They take advantage of the time with her father to be together and tell family stories that Tinkeleh fits together like pieces in a puzzle.

"A few weeks before holiday preparations began, more than 100 faithful arrived at the beautiful home of the Rabbi of Mezeritch," begins her father. "The rabbi didn't have many followers, just a few from the neighboring villages. It so happened that his daughter had married me, the Rabbi of Zbarash. I was considerably more liberal than he, which is why he didn't have as many followers as in times past.

"Nevertheless, a greater number of young people than had been expected came. Hasidim from cities as far off as Kiev or Lublin had arrived at the train station. Others, filled with an adventurous spirit, made the trip on foot, in cars or simply rented a truck among themselves. After a few glasses of liquor they formed a circle, embraced, and jumped up and down, singing like the Hasidim tend to do.

"In those days it wasn't at all common to see people walking. The cold had begun to set in and the fields, covered by a light frost, shone in the sun. With the news that great numbers of faithful were approaching the city, the inhabitants were brimming with excitement. The innkeepers hurried to straighten and clean the rooms, change the sheets, and take the wool mattresses stored in the attic out to air.

"Businesses washed their store windows and prepared new displays of their merchandise. The butcher had much work to do because he needed to slaughter more cattle following the kosher ritual. Fishermen took to the nearby lakes, seeing the opportunity for sales as large as those around the holidays.

"The whole town was making preparations for one of those special festivities that occur every once in a blue moon. The monotony of daily life gave way to a unique jubilation that each was taking advantage of in their own way.

"Even the church was participating in this reunion of the rabbi with his people. The sacristan, together with a few men, had cleaned the church, set out new candles, and dusted off books and old bibles. The faint winter light that filtered through the stained glass lent a joyous atmosphere to the place, concealing its dingy walls. The newly arrived and the sacristans greeted each other with a nod of the head:

"'Reb Hirsch Mitzner, it's been ages, scholem aleichem!' pronounced the sacristan.

"'Aleichem scholem, sacristan Joseph Smilenski,' Reb Hirsch replied merrily."

"The Rabbi of Mezeritch was not exactly a punctual man. The faithful were standing about wearing their phylacteries in that ceremonious way of the Hasidim, while others gathered in the small room next to the synagogue entrance to eat honey cake and drink tea from the recently polished samovar. The Hasidim, dressed in their long black coats, thin looking with dark eyes, and wearing thick glasses that gave them a crazed appearance, were filled with joy, ascetic and fervent in their prayers. The others, simple town folk and rabbis from the surrounding area, showed off their prosperity with expensive leather skullcaps and fine silk vests. Fat and rosy-cheeked, they chatted between prayers about their individual businesses. The poorest, dressed in their Sabbath clothes, took it all in with an attitude of joyful acceptance. Everyone was anxiously awaiting the rabbi."

The father interrupts his tale, lets out a slight sigh, and wipes his hand across his forehead, as if it pained him to remember.

"The rabbi, your grandfather, was tall and vigorous, with a long gray beard and bright, sharp gray eyes that let nothing of what was going on around him escape his notice. He wore white silk undergarments and fine leather shoes. The severe countenance that he always wore was the reflection of his thoughts: he never stopped thinking; whether he was brooding over something that troubled him or thinking about the evils of mankind, the sins of the children of Israel, the way that the Devil convinces Jewish boys to not study Torah, and the habits of certain Jewish women—among them his own daughter—who went around with young men, their arms bared in broad daylight, and their minds filled with the reading that led them away from Jewish faith and morals.

"How can this decay be avoided? Only a great tragedy, a great fire like that of Sodom and Gomorrah, could bring redemption.

He would be among God's chosen to witness the destruction from afar.

"When the rabbi entered the synagogue, the darkness of his own thoughts vanished into thin air. There, before him, was the Ark of the Law, the sacred books, the divine letters, warding off bad omens and the temptations of the gentile world. He gazed out on those present, covered his face with his hands, and slowly began to move to the rhythm of the prayers. He prayed for the unfaithful and sang for the faithful of Israel.

"The ceremony was interrupted only by several melodies followed by rapid murmurs, a mixture of praises and monologues. The Hasidim raised their heads every so often and their eyes filled with tears upon seeing the rabbi. In contrast, the humble townsmen, little used to such grand ceremonies, would sing out loudly and then suddenly stop to avoid being out of tune with the other voices.

"When the service was over the rabbi returned to his home; the travelers went to their lodgings, where they were met with soup, hot potatoes, egg pastries, and strong cherry liquor to comfort them. The townsfolk left to enjoy a holiday feast; herring served with potatoes in their skins and bread crusts with garlic spread.

"Every fireplace was lit, even though it wasn't really very cold.

"Once at home, your grandfather donned his blue silk robe with the yellow trim. He ate the meal of the wealthiest Jews in town, in which there was no lack of fresh bread, meat or fish, and he settled in next to the hearth absorbed in relentless thoughts that took him back and forth between God and Leviathan.

"I no longer remember how the enmity between your grandfather and me began. Surely it had to do with some Orthodox precept that didn't coincide with what the scholars maintained. The rabbi was not exactly a tolerant person. To him, I was 'that heretic who on top of everything had followers.' From the day Hannah married me she never saw her father again. I believe that she never really loved him."

As a matter of fact, the Rabbi of Mezeritch had been a tough, demanding, grumbling father only tempered by the good deeds of his wife, a woman more subdued than pious. The books she had devoured in secret along with a few free-thinking girlfriends saved Hannah from an arranged marriage to a young man in the congregation.

When Tinkeleh was born, Hannah and her husband resolved to bring her up as a sensible woman. So, when they discovered that she had a talent for painting, considered a sacrilege by religious Jews, they decided to support her in her dream of becoming an artist. They moved to Minsk to be able to send her to a better school.

Her father always says that Tinkeleh is the fruit of her mother's artistic sensibility and the respect that he always professed for the written word, pointing to himself proudly.

As the years passed, Tinkeleh's grandfather stopped practicing as a rabbi to dedicate himself to the study of Jewish philosophy and history. However, in spite of those changes, Hannah never reconciled with him. Permanently cut off from Mezeritch, she continues to suffer an emptiness that at times envelopes her in melancholy.

Deep in thought, Tinkeleh realizes that her mother still belongs to a world from which she can't completely separate herself. The sadness that Hannah sometimes manifests, and that

Tinkeleh doesn't want to make part of her own life, stems from that.

Will it be through form and color that she finds the necessary strength to face the dangers in the streets of Minsk that day to day snatch up people, to search for food, to see Menachem, to meet with Leah?

Yes, she promises herself.

6

I'm trying to climb a steep mountain and I keep slipping, until I awake drenched in sweat and curled up in a ball.

It's all real: the dreams and this cell.

Camila O'Gorman with her sex pierced by the scarlet red of the Rosas regime. Red, the color of guts and the gallows. Woman and lover. Whom did I abandon? Camila. I left her at the wayside and I, uneasy, am threatened by my own Rosas the Restorer on this side of a nameless pit.

What do the days matter when it's the minutes and seconds that have essence. The red seconds of scarlet pain.

Today I began eating a little more. Up until now my nausea was more overpowering than my hunger. Yes, one does become accustomed to everything. It's like being in a small ghetto, and if they could get through it in Europe I should be able to gather the strength to go on here. The bread is stale and the stew they feed us is a disgusting, sticky slop. It reminds me of stories that comrades who had completed their military service used to tell us. The filthy "rations" that caused them to have diarrhea for days and weeks on end.

Leap frog! Forward march! At ease! I smile at the orders I give myself and it feels like the corners of my mouth are cracking. How long has it been since I've laughed?

🌿 🌿 🌿

Is today Saturday?

It was on a Saturday, a long time ago, that I went to dance at the Tom and Jerry Club on José María Moreno and Rivadavia streets, with Ernesto. We had met at a birthday party and a few weeks later he asked me out. It was one of the few times I got up the nerve to go to one of those places. A record by Trío Los Panchos was playing, "wherever you go, if you remember me . . ."

We danced, holding each other closely, cheek to cheek, our chests and legs touching. "The sorrow that overcomes you . . ."

Music and cigarette smoke, cheap white wine, books, film directors, jazz, and art. And politics. Politics was like magic for Ernesto. It stuck to his body like glue. Smoke, body, militancy. Advancing like an armed soldier. He thought and he danced. He thought all the time.

His dance moves are a little clumsy but sensual. "Turning into the sun . . ."

I feel him on me and I have to contain myself to keep from melting like candle wax. So I go to the bathroom, splash water on my neck and face and then return. After a "romp" like that one, dawn would find me wrapped in a wrinkled sheet, damp from the thick liquid between my legs that I hold in, trembling, not wanting to wake up.

"Fatal love exists no more, a mere memory it will be . . ."

The voice of Johnny Albino at Tom and Jerry's and here in this cramped room.

"Desire is a guttural sound," I wrote in a poem the following day.

One caress and the world is moved.

I realize that I am attracted to what's different, and Ernesto

is just that. A man of action along with a sketcher of words. Do
I keep him separate from my daily routine? Risk mixed with the
forbidden excites me.

Risk, audacity. I move forward in her silence that reopens
wounds. The kind of wounds that don't leave scars.

Corín Tellado first, Simone de Beauvoir next, a little Erica
Jong, and Sylvia Plath later on. These are women who guided
me in certain directions. And so many others out there, waiting
to leave the printed word and become flesh. A slight glance, a
company of women that scale me like the steep mountain in my
dream. I went along gathering them up without realizing it, with
an animal instinct based on our common sex that unites us in
what we are beyond sex. Inhabited blood, I tell myself. Inhabited
by them. They are versions that I propose: "A hole, a trembling
wall . . . ," rants Pizarnik, an Alejandra in my daydream.

Around the time of Tom and Jerry's I stopped believing in that
God who dwelled inside the synagogue doors and who people
kissed on the holidays. An obvious God who ceased to interest
me. I exchanged the harshness of Jehovah for the harshness of
political activism.

I was active in everything: in politics, in my literary convictions, in atheism, in my relationships with others, in sex. I
became proud and determined and I hid as best I could my most
vulnerable spots during our nocturnal outings, sneaking into a
guarded area, being the look-out for some caper, taking the gun
off a policeman. It was gradual, very gradual. Routine and exciting. It was a good adrenaline rush, they used to say. To act like a
soldier, with the same vocation for obedience and command.

🌿 🌿 🌿

Does the Sabbath exist in this ghetto? Is it a ghetto or an extermination camp?

Is this my Saturday night body, stuck to the voices of the Los Panchos trio, which rises from the sticky floor?

Are these my hips dancing to the beat of a bolero with a Godless soul and yet with a predetermined destiny?

Los Panchos, Lucho Gatica, Johnny Mathis, Los Cinco Latinos. All of them corny as hell. They're for ditzy romantics, my schoolmates used to say, who were all crazy over the awful Rolling Stones. I was a fan of The Beatles. Their music seemed to come from another galaxy, even though they spoke English, which back then had begun to be a bad word for us. I didn't adore them as much as I did Mozart, "Bird," or Joplin, but they moved me in spite of the negative comments made about them by some of my friends at the time, young bookworms who read James Joyce, Mallarmé, and Lorraine. We shared lengthy conversations in the bars along Corrientes Avenue during which we changed the world several times never failing to quickly run through authors, movies, and musical topics in a catalog where the how mattered more than the why.

We'd meet up, I think, to go over our latest acquisitions. The person who got left out felt banished into an exile from which they could emerge gracefully the next week.

"The sorrow that overcomes you, turns into the sun," bellows the lyrics of the Los Panchos.

Ernesto asks in my ear if I like Gershwin, while he presses his right leg "there" and I place his arm across his chest to intercept him like I was taught to keep him from going too far and thinking that you are that kind of girl.

I'm familiar with Verdi, Tchaikovsky, Sarasate, and many others. But he has to ask me about Gershwin?

I smile at the memory and everything aches beneath this black cloth whose darkness keeps away the night.

I'm going to try and sleep. I sense that I don't have a lot of time and I need to save up my strength for what's coming.

"Fatal love exists no more . . . my memory will be . . . glowing in your nights," whispers Johnny Albino in my ear like a scratched record. "Where . . . ever . . . you go . . ."

Night time approaches.

7

Minsk, December 1941.

People are being taken off the streets daily and so Tinkeleh seldom goes out. Resignation has settled in like a habit and people are weary from hunger and frightened by what they don't understand, or refuse to understand. What's happening to them is too strange. They were familiar with pogroms, the ancestral anti-Semitism of the Poles, Cossacks pillaging and killing, but they sense that this is something darker and even more sinister.

When her father spoke to her about Hitler for the first time he didn't believe that the war would come so quickly or under these circumstances. He didn't even seem to understand when Tinkeleh told him what Leah's parents were advising, or he didn't want to understand. He began detaching himself from the years spent with a God that he'd inherited and for some time had accepted with resignation. It's true that he had been a rabbi different from the rest, and moving to a city like Minsk allowed him the opportunity to rid himself of the ancestral load he was carrying. Nevertheless, fatalism pervaded him and he couldn't avoid feeling that he was part of a tragic destiny that had been handed on to him like a legacy.

It's not easy getting news around town these days, but her father finds a way to keep up with what's going on, an ability he learned from his mother, Rivka, a restless woman who pondered over everything in search of answers. That's why Tinkeleh's father can't accept the apparent senselessness of recent events. They say that trenches are being dug in Warsaw and that the whole city is blacked out at night. The Germans are already in Czechoslovakia, but he insists that it will be nearly impossible for them to cross the Russian border.

He insists that they won't dare take on Russia. Just look at the example of Napoleon, and yet his voice trembles when he says it aloud with what little conviction his fear allows and which grows dimmer day by day as more bad news arrives.

She often slipped away to get a look at the Catholic weddings that were held outside the Jewish neighborhood. She was drawn to those hardy young men dressed in white silk shirts and bright pants who emerged from the church and climbed into carriages adorned with flowers and pine boughs, lifting women by the waist as their flowery skirts waved in the breeze.

In the yards between the houses they set up long tables covered with white tablecloths, bottles of vodka, potatoes prepared in every imaginable way, chick peas, and toasted semolina. Metallic grays and blues and the aroma of the pines pierced the darkness like the engravings of English impressionists she so enjoyed.

Tinkeleh imagines her next painting, the title of which is going to be "Village Celebration" and she'll conceal the human figures with spots of different sizes and colors.

Lost in thought she barely hears her father's cries.

"Tinkeleh, Tinkeleh, the Germans have invaded Russia!"

"What?" she asks absentmindedly. The church music is ring-ing in her head, her thoughts still occupied by the bride and groom who are dancing mazurkas and polkas with no concern for what's happening elsewhere. He begins to weep.

The peasants are accustomed to invasions and while they are treated worse than by their own government on such occasions, the difference is scarcely noticeable. All of them demand that taxes be paid and that they work from sunup to sundown. They don't care for the Germans one bit, actually they abhor them, but they also don't like the Jews who, it seems, the Germans are coming to put in their place. That is to say, the Jews are intruders themselves who take work away from the peasants, don't frequent their businesses, and they even have their own holidays, customs, and delicacies. They don't drink, they marry only amongst themselves and on top of that they live in better houses. Maybe the Germans are willing to do what the peasants don't have the stomach for.

Tinkeleh embraces her father in silence and they cry together for the first time.

8

Minsk, March 1942.

The months passed quickly from the night the Germans invaded Russia until their arrival in Minsk and the establishment of the work camps.

Her father is taken early every morning together with Russian peasants and other Jews who march in silence until they reach the woods to cut down trees. Tinkeleh, lying in bed in the attic hears them leave. She wants to escape and told her father so. He shook his head, resigned. Silent and growing thinner by the day, he leaves each morning to meet his fate without protest.

She and Hannah never leave the house. They only scurry into the streets to bring back firewood, potatoes, and beans that the neighbors sell to them for money. It's almost always she who takes the risk. She hides between the houses, looks about, and scampers for food to survive on. Two months ago a group of Jews were executed in the woods, not even their families speak of it. It's rumored there were more than one hundred.

It's only with Leah that she finds a moment to dream and talk about places they'd go or how they would exchange their clothes for the shorter, tighter-fitting ones they'd seen at the movies. They love the movies, but they can no longer go. Before

the executions they would save enough coins over several weeks
to go and buy sweets from non-Jewish stores that still sold such
things. They knew they were taking a risk, but it was the closest
thing they found to compare to their outings of times past. Since
the executions, though, it was as if they, the thousands of Jews in
Minsk, had never known any existence other than fear, hunger,
and uncertainty.

When they get the chance to escape the house they run
toward the woods holding hands, lifting each other's spirits,
laughing and short of breath, so as not to feel the terror knotted
in their throats.

She saw them today. She observed how they unloaded them from
the trucks. Old men, children, some women that she recognized
from the market, and Menachem's sister. They took them to
an enormous pit that the Jews themselves had dug several days
before. "The Jewish slaves," Tinkeleh calls them. Her mother gets
angry when Tinkeleh uses the word "slaves," but she sees her
father's agreement in his eyes, now smaller and more removed
from this world every day.

She heard someone shout, "*Shema Israel!*" a shriek of "*Got
mainer*" tore from the throat of an old woman, cries from a child
clinging to his mother's skirt, from Menachem's sister, frightened
with her head lowered as they were forced to squeeze together
side by side, some fallen on top of others. Almost none of them
cried. Only a baby held to his mother's breast who between sobs
sang "*schvartze oign, schvartze tzepelej*," black eyes, black braids.

When the machine guns started to fire, the dust in the middle of the field became a cloud of red and black mist that floated thickly on the afternoon air.

She goes up to her loft and sketches furiously. She scratches out page after page like a madwoman. "I still have Leah, Menachem, and my parents," she thinks.

9

To earn money I would give talks and conduct literary work-shops. I loathe teaching, but I didn't have many alternatives. It was a job that allowed me mobility, flexible schedules, and the constant possibility of transfers, which at this point in the game was essential.

The first time I was asked for advice I was dumbfounded. To feel recognized as an authoritative voice on literary matters some-how embarrassed me.

Deborah was the first to seek my guidance. She was around twenty years old, with long straight hair and big blue eyes. She didn't know whether to pursue a career as an author or a soap opera actress. She's of the kind that overpopulated Buenos Aires during these years: from a well-to-do family that wishes the best for their daughter, whom they've ordered not to look to closely at what goes on around you, and not get involved, because that won't help get you ahead in this world. She obeys them, but she's also interested in my opinions, which of course differ from those of her parents.

Her classmates viewed her with resentment and a bit of envy that led to a certain vanity on her part, which in turn led to a negative first impression of her.

When she came to me for advice she awaited my response, all

the while seductively moving her thick lips that she knew were attractive.

I told her to stay with her boyfriend and to work in television, which surely would end up being more gratifying and rewarding than writing.

Do we really give a damn about anyone else, especially one so different, so unfamiliar? May some Madame Curie save us! We play the role of "what we should be," but it's nothing more than a role. Training people to wear masks and assume roles. Artists, professionals, businessmen, we all form part of the same group of tightrope walkers where each one balances precariously on a wire stretched over the abyss called reality.

The things I think of in this place?

I sound like a silly petit-bourgeois girl. The one with an explanation for everything. The one who needs to sail along both shores at the same time.

That damnable habit of never taking a firm stand on anything. It's not suitable for a real militant.

But I did have my period of always, never, everything. Ultimately, sometimes became an anomalous life experience for me.

Sincerity is a dangerous thing. Telling someone about his lack of talent, or her banality. Admitting to ourselves our lack of talent, our banality. Confessing, for example, that the revolution seems like a sacred collective exercise to attain transcendence. But that's all bunk. I don't always (always?) think this way. Each answer, each definition, comes out like an act of commitment. Each hesitant gesture, each frustrated expectation, each dissimulation, was an attack against revolutionary duty.

Yes, I am a somewhat naïve silly petit-bourgeois who believes herself to not have been as systematic in my thinking as the others. I'm a dreamer who sometimes adopted narrow lines of thinking in order to subsist within a structure such as this, because one can't survive otherwise. The revolution demands difficult sacrifices from us. That part that I need to have secure, exact, without petit-bourgeois weaknesses, as we tend to label all those who don't think the same as we do.

We are the photo we carry around in a frame, with a smile looking toward posterity. Is posterity within the grasp of our resolve?

Where is my resolve now? With Tinkeleh or with Eva?

If Tinkeleh only knew the anger she provoked in me with her habit of hiding the past . . . She couldn't imagine it, and perhaps knowing it now, under these circumstances, would be unbearable for her.

Would she have broken the silence if she could have foreseen my choices? I spend these long hours, these unending nights piecing together my own puzzle, among screams, odors, memories, silences, and stares. Tinkeleh and Rita. The central figures in this painting, but in the background, deep into the canvas, one can catch a glimpse of the shadows of those other women.

This ghostly, empty space is populated by women.

I remember the dust that floated over the houses in April, almost all of them grey or whitewashed. Few cars went by in the afternoon, which heightened the sense of a pleasant autumn monotony.

I had a daily routine with a slow pace and routine that fascinated me. Above all if I came across a neighbor who, without saying a word, greeted me with a slight nod of the head. That closeness to an everyday occurrence that I so desperately sought after. A desperation disguised as indifference.

By five in the afternoon the owner of the pharmacy would usually be unoccupied and counting, as usual, the paradise bushes along either side of the sidewalk making sure that one hadn't disappeared at the hands of some allergy-suffering neighbor. I had the vague hope that he hadn't seen me, or that he hadn't recognized me with my new bobbed hairstyle, but he'd been eyeing me since the previous block with the stare of a medieval inquisitor. He was tilting his head back and forth as if to hide the stupor produced by drinking gin at that hour of the day. The same flabby face, the same slobbery smile, the same eyes charged with rancor that I remembered from his father and which he inherited along with the pharmacy.

He always stopped me with some stupid question and I would answer back with something equally as dumb just to play along. The predictable dialogues were one of the things I liked most about the neighborhood.

Why do these memories come back to me and others remain buried?

In this place of cruelty, this shapeless place, without trees or butterflies or anyone to direct a human gaze toward, a sensual blow at moments shakes my very soul. Strapped to the iron table, wet, thirsty, and sore, I am entirely body and words.

Vehicles drive by outside. I hear them. I can almost touch them in the cold night. They are part of an audible landscape that is familiar to me. A place different than this one, a place where people exist.

A horrendous scream is heard that severs my contact with the world. I am alone against that scream and I detest the acrid stench of helplessness.

The sound of the screeching tires on the asphalt still echoes in my head. Arms hoisted me into the air like a ball and tossed me into the truck. I bounced on the metal floor and there was an infinitely long ride during which I thought of my mother, in another truck, on another road, in another place, but with the same violence. She in Minsk headed toward Terezin and I in Buenos Aires headed . . . where?

A caste of murderers. The Nazis gassed, starved, humiliated. Here they insult, torture, rape. Caste of murderers. I hear them laugh, gamble, drink . . . Am I there or here?

The foul stench is part of this place. I wear it stuck to my skin like a curse, like a yellow star.

They need alcohol to defend the Western world from women like me. A caste of murderers that grind and crush with fury. I listen to them and they to me.

"How is this night different from all other nights?" We would read gathered together at Passover dinner to remember our enslavement in Egypt. "How is Tinkeleh different than I?" I think on this night that is not Pessach and where there is no Seder.

"Being woman is like the grass," I wrote in my black oilskin notebook, "moist and unknown."

What am I playing at? Woman among women in revolution. The revolution of Rivka, Tinkeleh, Hannah. The revolution of Evita who shall return and be millions.

Will we, her millions, return?

I scratch through the pain to find my women. Among the odor of rancid wine and urine I pursue them so that I can climb a tree and stay there. Like Calvino's "Baron in the trees" I'll become the "woman in the trees." Observing, in silence and freedom. From there I'll discover little by little what Tinkeleh kept hiding from me.

Should we have changed the questions asked during Pessach? Demand that she answer them?

That Tinkeleh who, the moment she stepped off the ship, hid herself forever.

I am the daughter of your silence.

How am I different, Tinkeleh, from you?

I dragged myself through the desert where I prayed for manna and it rained stones.

But the path, your path, does not lead to my Promised Land. I only harbor questions like on the Passover of absent relatives, of cousins exchanging glittery cardboard figures.

A last supper upon this iron table with several Judases spitting in my face.

I submerge myself in your milk without *yerba mate*. I attack like a lion crouching on the steppes. I listen and I keep quiet. Like you in me. They won't get a word out of me. Only your heavy sigh that belongs to me now.

Got alein veist! I shout at the devils.

10

Cigarettes. I miss them so much.

I started smoking at a very young age. It was my second year of high school when the girl who sat next to me showed up with a pack of imported filtered Parliaments that had been given to her. "They're the best," she said. In the beginning I was disgusted by the hot smoke flowing through my nose and throat that burned like fire. Over time that burning turned into a caress, the caress into pleasure, the pleasure into an urgent need.

When I had the money I bought Parliaments, but then I changed to Jockey Club, after that to Le Mans lights. When someone traveled abroad I would ask for the More brand. They were like chocolate, kind of sweet. But if someone offered me a Chesterfield, I didn't turn it down.

Smoking gave me the same buzz as a Noel chocolate and peanut candy bar that I used to get when I'd go to the neighborhood movie house on "Ladies Day" to see three movies for eighty cents.

It's very difficult for someone who's never smoked to understand what it means, not to mention the loyalty to a brand, an aroma, a certain kind of puff, a way of exhaling the smoke, the different ways to light up.

It's just another form of suffering now, without that flavor in my throat, in my gut, that taste that becomes attuned to your body and becomes a kind of consummation.

Years went by before I adopted Marlboros permanently. They were stronger and more flavorful than any others I tried before. I christened them the "perfect smoke."

My life for a Marlboro! How I miss you, dear ol' cig. I no longer know if it's the smoking or the ritual that I dream of through many nights: taking the pack out my pocket, selecting a cigarette, drawing it to my lips, lighting it and taking the first few puffs, like wanting to drink in the world. Feeling at that moment that I am unique, fulfilled, removed from everything else.

People for whom smoking isn't a passion could never feel the pain that quitting it creates in your body.

Some comrades who were out-and-out fanatics criticized it as a capitalist vice. I let them go on about it, because deep down I believed that it was like sex: whoever hasn't felt the jolt of an orgasm isn't qualified to give classes on chastity.

The person who doesn't smoke and doesn't derive pleasure from the impact of the smoke in the lungs, the person who renounces a basic belief, whatever it may be, and who doesn't devote themselves—to Che, to Evita, to Mao, to something or someone—is not likely to comprehend what it feels like to smoke, to fight for an ideal or a mouthful of words uttered in the wind. They are the signs of a strength that I get from my mother, and that she believed she buried in her silence; the traces of an energy that I see in myself. It didn't get lost in the emptiness of the everybody, the many, the future, the Argentine final blow, that final act in which we are going to make the Americas Peronist: with San Martín in our heart, Bolívar at the rear, Perón at the head, and Evita in our soul.

Only having a smoke could give any meaning to my struggle right now.

11

Minsk, May 1942.

She doesn't know how long she's been here.

The stench of onion and rancid potatoes is making her sick, but there's nothing in her stomach to vomit up even if she felt like it.

What could have happened to her mother? Did they load her onto a different truck?

A week ago the men didn't come back from work. They took them directly from the camp. Her father was among them.

Tinkeleh closes her eyes tightly wanting not to cry. She remembers the last time that he told her one of those stories he was fond of sharing with her, in which real people were mixed up with fictional adventures and episodes that got them both to laughing out loud.

In those days—she covers her ears so that she can hear her father's voice—the earth was not as we know it today. It was all steppes, ice, and silence. The mountains sprang from the bowels of the earth, enormous gashes opened on plateaus from which frozen rocks emerged. There was no plant life to be found on the windswept plains and a dark and eternal winter fell upon the land, bringing death to all living things. Those who didn't find shelter in crags, frozen trunks, and caves perished. Those who hadn't yet discovered fire, who couldn't find food, or cover their bodies with skins died. Even the plants and animals. Only the youngest and strongest warriors were able to resist the inclement conditions. Among them was Aruch, most likely the forebear of the Ur clan, a group of nomadic hunters that would become the tribe from which it is believed Abraham, our patriarch, could have come.

Aruch lived near the Dead Sea, or what was later the Dead Sea, in a cave made from a pile of stones at the base of mountain that protected him from the ice. He hunted animals that came to the frozen surface in hope that it would melt into water. It had been days since the cracking ice had kept the few surviving animals from approaching. I'll have to abandon this place or I'll die, thought Aruch.

He covered his body with grease as protection from the cold and clothed himself in several fur hides. He loaded up the few strips of dried meat he had left, hung his tools and hunting implements on his belt, and tried to walk along the borders of ice which seemed to be more stable. As he went along, hungry animals began to stalk him. They were skinny, almost emaciated, they all looked the same, and they dragged themselves along without the strength to attack him.

He walked along the shore of the frozen sea leaving behind him the most dangerous stretch until nightfall. Facing the glare of those specters that were still accompanying him, he struck two stones together over a mound of dried grass that he kept in his leather pouch and soon a small flame arose out of nowhere. He took a strip of meat and chewed it slowly until all that was left was the hide, which he tossed to his traveling companions. More hungry than he, the animals swallowed it quietly as if taking care not to waste their strength and every once in a while they gave him a look of gratitude.

He didn't count how many moons he'd been walking, but he felt the fatigue in his legs and his shoulders that had begun to hunch over. The animals that followed him began to die off without his noticing. There remained only a small wolf, all skin and bones, that didn't have the strength even to lift its head.

The wolf and he stared at one another, as if trying to guess which would be the first to turn on the other. Aruch thought several times about attacking it, but couldn't bring himself to do it. Perhaps they were the only two living things left in all the land.

He chewed on mosses and lichens scraped from a cave that, protected from the cold, still had traces of vegetation. He walked very little since he was almost entirely drained of energy.

But one morning, a rustle at first and then a bang awoke him. The sun returned to the earth after having been hidden for a long time and it was melting the ice flows in the valley. Water began to run; cold, pure water than trickled down the cracks in the ice. He assumed that it was the work of the gods. Though he didn't like asking things of them, he knew they existed, and maybe that's why they remembered him and the wolf.

Tinkeleh dozes off, completely unaware of the train car she was in or the weeping that every now and then interrupted the relentless sound of the wheels on the track. She suddenly feels protected by those same gods that, like with Aruch, won't forget about her.

From that spot—says her father continuing the tale—Aruch walked and walked until he found a suitable place where the hunting and the gathering of other men and women who were also emerging from the eternal winter would allow them to share a special strength that he recognized in himself. From that will to persist, to join in a community of survival, rose Abraham, and he came to us—states her father proudly.

"Is it so written?" she asked him wryly.

"I don't know if it is written so, but if it wasn't Aruch, it would have been someone else like him who lit the way for us from those days up to our time."

He had ceased his daily practice of reading the Bible and the Talmud, but like the majority of people, he loved the stories of the Hasidim. Treating them like legends and stories, he spiced them up with quotes and annotations from the Kabala.

She opens her eyes wide in order to determine if what she's thinking is a dream or if what's happening to her is a dream. The smell, the murmurs, Leah's hand squeezing her own so that they feel close together, all bring her back to reality and cause her pain.

Later, still holding hands, they are unloaded into an empty train station and pushed inside a train car that begins to fill up with men, women, and youngsters.

Outside there is a line of trucks from which people are being shoved. Those who fall down get back up quickly and climb onto the train. She tries to find her mother, but the crowd is a faceless mass moved along by orders, shouts, and shoves.

She remains in the doorway of the car for an instant, nothing more than a figureless background in that grotesque landscape.

12

Terezin, 1942.

When she arrives at Terezin she keeps her own clothes since there are not yet enough uniforms returned from the front. She also gets to keep a small bag with a few belongings and a little wooden bench that her father made for her.

Terezin, the lovely citadel that had been built in the seventeenth century in honor of the Empress Maria Therese, is now a walled fortress that allows for practically no contact with the outside. In just a few days, Tinkeleh is able to make a mental map of the buildings. The entrance opens onto the administrative block and the office of arrivals where all the prisoners' belongings are confiscated. Then, to the guard station, where they are questioned and accounted for, and near there, the office of Commandant Heinrich Jöckel. Beyond there, the clothing warehouse where the newly arrived surrender their own clothes in exchange for military uniforms taken from defeated armies.

Through the entry gate with the sign reading *Arbeit Macht Frei* (work shall set you free) you enter the first block, where 1,500 prisoners are housed. Nearby, the infirmary and the bathroom with the delousing center. There is also an examination room with its respective doctors, and almost at the very end there is the hospital, very close to the cadaver depository. A little farther on, the gallows, the mass graves, and the door of death, through which prisoners pass on the way to be executed.

In the main block there is a swimming pool for the guards and their families, a cinema, and the administrative area, called Block IV. In the group cells there are between 400 and 600 people housed together. At a distance, the SS barracks and in front, the commandant's house. Block II is where the prisoner workshops are, and the officers' club.

The Camp commandant enjoys a great many luxuries and entertains himself with a variety of cruel acts, which he carries out with a passion: he rapes and humiliates young girls, and walks among the prisoners kicking them at random. When he gets drunks he plays "target practice" with them.

In the beginning Tinkeleh, anguished and fearful, refuses to make friends with anyone. The last days in Minsk flash through her mind and drain the energy she needs to survive. Several young girls approach her. They are girls who've been at Terezin longer and who know the tricks to avoid getting to the point that no one wants to mention: the final transport. Everyone knows that you have to eat whatever you can get, you can't get sick, and if possible, you have to demonstrate an ability for hard labor so that you don't get placed among the disposable, which is what happens to the elderly and the children.

Tinkeleh lives in a barracks with a group of women and Leah. They sleep on a hard, dirty cot where fleas are habitual residents.

In spite of it all, incredibly, there is something positive: she never imagined she would meet such a large number of such diverse people. They come from Bohemia, Moravia, Denmark, Hungary, Holland and so many other countries and cities that she had only heard about because her father talked about them with great admiration, repeating what his mother Rivka had once told him.

Food is scarce and hunger is a constant torment. They are served a black coffee-like liquid for breakfast. At noon, bread and barley soup, and at night a sticky liquid in which a chunk of potato or two is floating. Many kids wander around by themselves trying to beg for food with that sad, austere look that sticks in their eyes like a disease.

She's amazed that, in spite of the misery, there is a theater, a classical music orchestra, and children and young people learn to paint and draw. Teachers, scientists, and artists lead discussions and give classes to help one bear up under the agonizing reality.

Many orphans are housed in the *heim*, homes supervised by teachers that operate in large rooms behind the backs of the SS.

Games are organized for the younger kids in the patios, barracks, and old houses. Their parents, like Tinkeleh's, were taken to other locations and they quickly adapt to begging for food, hiding from the guards, or going around in small groups for protection. Those who don't adapt die of hunger or sadness, or they are simply hauled off. Over time they either see their friends taken away or they don't find them the next day. They hide expressions that are more of resignation than sadness because they have grown accustomed to losing loved ones. When new contingents arrive, they welcome them cordially and they teach them the basic unwritten laws of survival. They try to place them with groups of youngsters with similar interests or they take the youngest ones to the teachers' classes, grouping them by language or age.

Over the following days, Tinkeleh tries to recover the images

of her father, who at night whispers anecdotes and stories in her
ear, like the story of Purim or of Ur. She doesn't want to forget
his voice, nor his way of telling a story, nor his own story that she
pieces together with a bravery that gives her more strength than
what little food she manages to consume.

She imagines him, like so many times, seated near the fire
telling her about Rivka, a woman of strong character and thinking
ahead of her time, who counseled the young people in the village
who went to her for advice on different matters. She was not like
other rabbis' wives; what's more, she found it difficult to meld
her vocation for the world and people with religious orthodoxy,
but she managed to do it. She even went several times to Kiev
and Odessa because she liked to travel, discover, and delve into
other realities. "Jews need to get out of these villages and discover other worlds," Rivka would demand. "People are all alike,
but big cities have more things to offer than one ever imagined
and they teach one to think differently." That's what Tinkeleh's
grandmother was like, her father's mother, whom she never knew.
She thinks about her grandmother, so much stronger than her
own mother, and she needs them to care for her and help her to
gather all the strength she can in order to not give up.

She enjoys painting, listening to music, reading; but above all
painting. There are wonderful teachers and others here to guide
her. She meets up with other boys and girls on Pieval Street, in
an old scrap hangar, or sometimes in a barracks when the group
was taken out to work, or in places temporarily uninhabited
between the transport of one group of prisoners and the arrival of
another contingent.

In the old hangar there is an abandoned piano that with a few rudimentary instruments a Russian tuner managed to get working.

They meet at times when the guards are in the club or busy with administrative duties, and with whatever each of them was able to rescue they improvise chamber concerts, where lyric singers sometimes participate. To Tinkeleh, who never left her hometown, it all seems so marvelous that at times she forgets where she is. Young and old alike happily get together for these moments of small delights, for a brief reunion with the world.

They seek out schedules for love also. In the beginning she was amazed that couples formed so quickly there, but with time she came to understand that despair, loneliness, and fear combine to share what no one can take from them for now: bodies, beating hearts, kisses on lips that are cracked but hungry for human warmth.

They draw, they paint, they exchange what few materials each could carry with them from home. In those brief moments, she feels happy. Sometimes they bring her poems or a letter for her to read and then draw a few lines of color on the page, because they can receive and send letters to relatives, although since they never get answered, Tinkeleh suspects that in reality the letters probably never go beyond the commandant's house, or like in own her case, there is no one left to answer.

13

Terezin, September 1942.

She misses the music of the song birds in Minsk. Here the birds don't sing. People slip by, they don't walk; they murmur, instead of talk; they resign themselves, they don't ask questions. But, alongside the despair are others who quietly resist, like Gideon Klein, who once again prepares to play the piano with those long fingers that have not lost their dexterity. "You're like Beethoven, with furrowed brow like a cloud before it rains," David, a young man whom Gideon reminds of his native Prague, tells him. Even though an instrument sounds, though an aria is sung or beautiful paintings are created, silence is what thrives most in the Camp. Silence and terror.

Camp is a word that Tinkeleh says almost as often as "bread" or "water." It's important to know the Camp.

What can and can't be done in the Camp.

Where you can walk in the Camp, and where you cannot.

With whom you can talk and from whom you should hide in the Camp.

Who writes in the Camp.

Who sings in the Camp.

Who paints in the Camp.

Who steals in the Camp.

Who reports you in the Camp.

Who dreams in the Camp.

Who survives in the Camp.

Camp: fraternity, overcrowding, dispossession, art.

To sit in front of the walls or roam through every tiny space, count the giant rocks, cross the patios whenever you can, while the moss covers the walls and you watch it grow like a nightmare. Some walk through the streets looking for something to eat, muttering words in their native language. Others, younger, hope to find a dead person to take his coat or boots. Each one follows an internal mandate that allows him to live for one more day. Those who can't go on let themselves die.

In these times, Terezin begins to be populated by different voices. Long trains head out for unknown places and take with them numbers of people chosen at random off the street, from houses, or at meeting places. Sometimes others arrive with new contingents who for a short period of time make contacts or generate certain hopes.

She asks those who have recently arrived from Minsk or the surrounding areas if anyone knows what happened to her parents. She expects to hear that they're at the place no one names, for which they feel a kind of curiosity and fear, and where she knows she'll be headed someday.

Meanwhile, she meets with the teacher, with her schoolmates, and Leah.

There are several groups with different teachers set up in places that are out of the view of the guards. Teachers and pupils keep circulating in and out because of the transports.

They meet because of common interests or because someone

takes them to a particular meeting. She and Leah quickly sign on for the classes taught by Professor Liebschtein. Perhaps because it's a group in which painting and literature are combined with philosophical discussions where everyone can give their opinion freely on the meaning of existence. They found a room with unused military clothing. They form the clothes into piles and sit on them like they were benches. In addition, all that cloth absorbs the sound of their voices making it more difficult to hear each other. Only occasional prisoners go there to pick out clothes when the "greenies" arrive in Camp.

When a member stops attending no one asks why.

Leah, who had always been so enthusiastic and talented, has little by little been losing her creative vitality. Without her parents, she is one more inconsolable orphan in Terezin.

During this time a typhus epidemic is spreading, and the malnourished and depressed are the first to catch the contagion. The hospital for Jews is filling up with the infirm and they are beginning to send the dead to the crematorium that just began operation. The stench and smoke have stuck to her body like a shadow she can't shake.

Tinkeleh desperately tries to care after Leah. She's worried by her progressive lack of interest and also her need to tightly clutch the only thing that remains of her past, her memories. She knows that such an attitude is a voyage with a foreseeable end, but she can only do so much. She's barely got enough strength to keep herself going. Avoiding the transports, managing to find a few scraps left by the guards to feed them both, secreting away clothes taken from Pieval Street for the coming winter, gathering the strength to paint something, and being grateful under her breath that her good health has saved her from typhus. She hates to think it, but her friend, with whom she's been able to share almost nothing this week, has become a burden that is pushing her unwillingly toward a dark place that she tries to elude on a daily basis.

14

I am covered, gagged, infected, accused, filed away, and buried.

"Ring around the rosy, pocket full of posies, ashes, ashes, we all fall down."

"Angel of death, come unto me." Children's games in which senseless words take on a prophetic meaning. Then and now. "Ashes, ashes, we all fall down." I want to go to him, guardian angel come to me; or be Queen Esther and decide my life or my death like on Purim.

Free me from my enemies, unmask them and hang them in my place, like King Ahasverus who saved the Jews from the noose. On Purim my father would recount the saga of the Jewish victory in Persia. Queen Esther was a beautiful Jewish woman, and the king fell in love and married her. The Prime Minister, known as Aman the Cruel, designed a plot to kill all the Jews in the kingdom. She, assimilated through her role as queen, and under the counsel of her uncle Mordechai, a faithful Jew, managed to convince her beloved husband to hang the treacherous minister instead of the Jews.

My father's stories preserve the warmth of a tradition that unites me with my people. Even Israel, to which my father is devoted and in another time I had embraced with passion but

today define as "the capitalist-ogre-aggressor-of-the-Middle-East."
But I can't completely banish it from my affections. It hurts him
to hear that from me. It hurts me to not share with him those
things that brought us together, but between betraying Israel to
my father and betraying Israel for the cause I have no choice.

"Ring around the rosy, pocket full of posies, ashes, ashes, we all
fall down."

Queen Esther, Israel, my father, Moses, lines that slice the
night into pieces in order to remember: Am I what I was? Where
is the person that I am?

And life, little one, where is life headed?

I gave up my studies. I kept giving my classes and I was an activist, even though my activism comprised the core of my daily life,
it was also the forum for constant arguments with my mother.
She couldn't understand that what I was trying to do was for her
benefit also. I didn't tell her that and she wouldn't have believed
it anyway. She'll never know that it was she who unwittingly
forced my decision. Tinkeleh, with her veiled suffering, created a
festering wound in me.

It is not Purim and I am not Queen Esther. I also cannot, like
Samson, topple the columns of this Philistine temple. But I can
remember.

"Angel of death, come unto me," I say out loud, startling
myself.

I stare at one of the walls, my mirror during these times and
the anchor that grounds me to the world going on outside these
walls of blood and ash.

In the dampness I try to make out the blurred image of Elena. We're on a trip, traveling in third class, the aroma of jasmine and the flavor of ripe fruit.

Your time on earth is not over, woman. You chose one door but there are several yet to open. The faces foretell it. Elena is only a stop on the way.

Angel of death, do not come for me.

15

It begins like a silhouette of blurred lines, but once it penetrates the wall of the cell it becomes an unstoppable whirlwind.

I'm at the Bar Politeama. They consider me to be a "tough chick" though I rarely carried weapons and that seemed odd to the others, though not, of course, to Ernesto.

He suggested we go out on missions together to get my courage up, but it wasn't allowed, so they had to deal with the fact that I did more planning than bomb throwing. They accepted it because I remained firm in my convictions. I'm audacious in my proposals and daring with the actions I take. They know next to nothing about my sleepless nights. The doubts that eat holes in my stomach and the bitter taste that I can't celebrate as victory each time that the dead are labeled as "them" or "us." It was only with Ernesto that I managed to get a good night's sleep. Like with my father's stories, after being with him I could wake up rested and stress free.

Elena appears on my wall without asking. She's not an ordinary person, and neither is anything that happens to her. As always, I had to wait half an hour for her. She was pale as a ghost when she reached the table.

"I didn't tell you everything the other afternoon because I didn't have the ovaries for it," she said distressingly. At that moment an ambulance was going by on Corrientes, and the siren kept me from understanding what she was saying. Her lower lip that pulled to the left when she spoke was trembling. "Roberto makes me sick."

I thought I heard her incorrectly.

"He's a great guy in spite of his jealousy," she continued, "but for some time now I find him repulsive whenever he gets close." She took a deep breath. "I don't know what to do. After being together for five years, I can't bring myself to face the situation and I don't know what to say to break it off with him. It's horrible dumping someone you loved."

It was the same as with Haydée: when I was with Elena, my socialist morals were compromised and it confused me. Her transgressions appealed to me as much as passionate big-screen kisses. That kind of game tickled my hide. A hide that was improperly cured for such battles.

She loved being the strange anarchist. Although her knights were not always as valiant or as tortuous as she presented them to be. Rather, they were ambitious social climbers who, like Ramón—the recently acquired masseur—showed her a new and exciting world.

"I know that Roberto is going to kill me. He showed me a revolver that he carries with him and you know he'd be capable of it, because he suspects something in all that's going on," she continued.

I felt uneasy with a situation that I could no longer only view—as I preferred—through a keyhole. I decided to cut our meeting short. You might call my compulsion for drawing close to excitement only to vanish "Foreplay interruptus."

Since that meeting I kept evasive ties to Elena. I felt relieved when our contract with the Ministry of Education, where we both had administrative jobs, ended. I was able to distance myself, stop seeing her, much like I did less gracefully at the time with Haydée. The only dose of adrenaline I allowed myself I got from being an activist. I guess my relationship with Ernesto was part of the limited excitement I got from activism.

The wall-mirror reflects an indelible image of myself that frightens me. Most of the time I prefer to view myself in the reflection of the armor I use for protection, rather than the reflection of what I lack.

These days I'm coming to terms with the girl from Chacarita, the one who played marbles, kites, soccer in the neighborhood, and drank *yerba mate* with milk. I'm penetrating unanaesthetized into that harsh, bullet-proof person I've become.

I played boys' games. Woodshop instead of sewing, kite flying instead of embroidering, violin instead of piano.

The only doll I had was bald and I pushed her blue eyes into her skull. I kept her naked and blind and only took her out of the crib a few times. I never even gave her a name.

Naked, blind, and nameless. Just like now.

The pain of it pierces my body. It's not the pain of the electric prod. It's more intense, because I pierce my own soul. Seeing myself helpless and alone exposes my weaknesses.

Fear, too. It's been forbidden for so long to feel it, to speak of it, or for other comrades to show it. But something about that fear pleases me now. To realize that in some way they didn't completely erase the feelings that I tried to rid myself of. The feelings that my grandmother Hannah must have turned to when darkness overtook her life, or, I imagine, what Leah must have seen on that train that carried her toward the abyss.

Leah, Hannah, and Elena dance on my retina like the eyeless doll. No eyes, I repeat, and I shake like a dried branch about to snap in the wind.

16

I hadn't seen Elena since our time together at the Ministry and then by chance one day I ran into her.

She was wearing a tight skirt with a slit up the side that revealed her white, almost, milky skin; boobs bursting out of her low-cut blouse; stiletto heels, as was her style, and a vintage white purse. She had left those loose-fitting tops, ample floor-length skirts, and handcrafted sandals far behind. She looked radiant. I couldn't resist. "Do you have time for a coffee?" "Not really," she answered. "I'm actually on my way to a massage appointment in fifty minutes and I was passing by the book stores. But, why not? Just for a bit."

We went to the Politeama. We were only a few blocks from Paraná and Corrientes, but headed there out of habit.

With Haydée it had been La Giralda; with Elena, it was Politeama. "As usual, everything nice and compartmentalized in my life," I think.

We started off talking about family, relationships, and our currents jobs. It was difficult to talk about ourselves seriously. In this case, anyway, there wasn't a lot I could say. How could I tell her about my plunge into militant activism and the intensity of my involvement?

Elena's voice sounds like a recent, gentle echo and I love noticing the tilt of her mouth when she talks.

Her relationship with Roberto had ended in true dramatic fashion, with an attempted suicide on his part. He followed her. She quit her job. She stopped seeing her family, who were opposed to her splitting up with Roberto. She was grateful for not giving in to the temptation to have a normal family life, in the image and likeness of her parents. She spoke with very little inflection in her voice, which was odd for her, and she'd give pitiful little smiles when she mentioned Roberto.

"What else do you want to know?"

"You and Ramón."

"Look, Rita, if you're really interested, we'll continue with the next chapter another time," she stated ironically, "like I said, I have a client waiting."

We arranged to see one another the following week. I began to experience the same uneasiness as I had so many times before, and it provoked a strange melancholy in me.

Between the organizing, the secretiveness, and the violence of the last few months, Elena was like a voice from the great beyond.

I don't want to open my eyes because I know that the only thing there is the wall, dampness, a scream-proof heart, waste hidden in every corner. Why go on if Elena is still at the Politeama and I'm in here?

I arrive early, as always.

She ordered a gin on ice. I was surprised by her lack of good judgment and at the same time by my own prudishness: judging her for having a drink at this hour, like the activists she criticized would have done.

The expression on Elena's face had acquired an air of sharp mockery. Her dark, almost bulging eyes blinked rapidly as she herself seemed surprised by the stories she was telling. She wasn't one of those people who get together just to hear themselves talk. She was more intuitive, and she must have known that I was involved in things that I wasn't about to let spill out of my mouth. She also detected my enthusiasm for her tale.

"Well, everything I know I learned from Ramón. I knew nothing about life before meeting him. With Roberto, sex, pleasure, was like a kids' circle jerk, nothing but shared masturbation. What's more, I don't think either of us ever fantasized beyond the moment. We were two sweethearts with huge sex drives and very little imagination."

The words hit me like a slap in the face. I blushed, much to my chagrin. I thought of Ernesto, on the mattress on the floor, in a rush to mix pleasure with duty.

I can't distinguish between real pain and the pain of remembering.

I'm nauseated. The smell of the cheap oil in the stew the "fat man" gave me at noon as a Christmas present and Elena's voice are burning up half my body. If only I could calm down and sleep a little before returning to the Politeama with her.

Coffee, Elena, cigarettes: a confusion of pleasurable sensations that take me away from the place I'm in. I don't dare think about whether I'm going somewhere.

It's more like I can recognize that I come from various places, from various women, some real, others imagined: the rebellious one, the ironic one, the activist, the helpless one, the courageous one, the sensual one, the inflexible one, the rancorous one, the transgressive one.

To whom do I belong? Do I even belong to myself? Or does only the revolution define my identity?

Meanwhile, Elena's mouth appears before me mocking and defiant.

"I had gone only to get a neck massage. But once there, on the massage table, as soon as he touched me I realized that I wouldn't be able to withstand it. I began to sweat. He slowly massaged my arms and legs, until I felt like I was melting into a giant viscous blob and I was purring like a cat with a warm bowl of milk.

"Now, he taught me all the techniques he knew. My massages not only alleviate the soreness in muscles and bones, they rebuild you vertebra by vertebra until you discover who you are, beyond your skin and bones. It's an exercise that stimulates the recovery of vigor in places you least suspect. These massages are not for everyone. They can mortally wound you. Pleasure is a definitive sensation. You are what they are, what they want or what they turn you into. One or several, it doesn't matter.

"This is my revolution: Anarchist-Sensuality," she said with an ironic expression of pride on her face.

She blinked, looked straight into my eyes and waited. I felt like an idiot and couldn't utter a word. I took her hands in mine and stroked them gently. It wasn't a usual gesture, more like a fond good-bye. I sensed that would be the last encounter between the two of us. She gave a warm smile, titling her mouth tenderly she understood.

"Let me leave the tip," she said rising gently out of her seat as if to soften the blow of that strange good-bye.

I take the spoon from the lunch stew and scratch the names HAYDÉE / ELENA / RITA into the surface of the wall so that someone may know what each of my nights in this hole has been.

"The night was wide . . ." How did it go? "The night was wide and furnished scant / with but a single star / that often as a cloud it met / blew itself out for fear," wrote Emily. None other than Emily. Nothing other than Rita. The night is brutal . . . and ours alone, Emily.

I took a shower today and it seems ridiculous that such a simple pleasure could cheer up my afternoon.

It's also incredible that some practices are so similar to activist ideals. Cakes of lye soap, lukewarm water only, simple food and little of it. No shampoo, no soothing hot water, no attention to smells and flavors.

How are the ESMA (Navy School of Mechanics) and revolutionary morals alike? Am I crazy to compare them? Is it even possible to speak of these murderers and my comrades in the same breath?

"Fucking Nazis!" I scream out loud in an effort to clear the tangled webs clouding my brain.

"Fucking Nazis!" I scream again, getting no response. They're likely changing the guards since it's getting dark outside.

It's been days since they've taken me to the special room, but I don't get my hopes up. They're waiting for me to recover a bit before continuing their routine.

✴ ✴ ✴

I add RIVKA / HANNAH / TINKELEH to the carved names. They are part of an intimate story that I drag around like a chain. Elena and Haydée were one attempt, but I refused them or couldn't learn to fly like them. Rivka finds joy in the audacity that lives on in me, Hannah keeps the pain locked up, and Tinkeleh is this useless survival.

In here I am all of them. They are my revenge, my pleasure, my sentence.

Am I who I wanted to be? The one who entered immortality at 8:25? The protagonist of Terezin who returns at all cost? Or a yellow star faded by time?

RIVKA / HANNAH / TINKELEH

Fuck, I don't give a shit about immortality.

17

"Ring around the rosy, pocket full of posies . . ." I persist with my favorite game. It was a time of repeated tonsillitis attacks, high fevers, family secrets, and adventures in the streets blanketed in autumn leaves.

I'm about to turn twenty-eight. When I was seven, the country was going through one of its most violent periods, mostly in Córdoba and Buenos Aires. Airplanes roared low over the housetops and we were forced to evacuate the school hurriedly.

The fourth-grade teacher, who I didn't like at all, went from room to room in her muslin socks, button-up shoes, and long wavy hair pulled back, shouting with glee: They're bombing Plaza de Mayo!

"Ashes, ashes, we all fall down . . ." I'm overcome now with the same anguish my mother suffered from. She was disturbed by words like "revolution," "airplanes," "bombings."

My father wasn't a Peronist, but he wasn't an anti-Peronist either, like the majority of the Jewish community amongst whom Perón's record inspired distrust. He was cautious, but he most definitely belonged to the working class. He said Perón had helped them to be considered as people. On the inside he was grateful for the small things that he had achieved during the

Perón era: steady work, respect for his status as a wage-earner, a certain economic stability that he had never known before.

Contrary to Mother, he would have left the country for good but he wasn't able to make the dream of settling in Israel come true. He had great admiration for the work carried out by pioneers who drained all the swamps dressed in blue and white. He idealizes everything that happens there and he lives as if his life depended more on the survival of Israel than of Argentina. On the other hand, for my mother Israel is a fantasy land, an idealization created by my father. The mere thought of going through another uprooting produces such a panic in her that she flat out refuses to reconsider the topic.

She lives in a type of chest, hidden away under lock and key to which no one has access.

The afternoon of the revolution, I'd climbed the shelves where she kept boxes of old documents and discovered a faded yellow star among drawings of different sizes.

I don't know if I understood then just what she was hiding there, but something startled me, a secret that I shouldn't violate but that I knew I was a part of. I impatiently left the star in its place with the feeling that I was committing a sacrilege that Tinkeleh wouldn't forgive.

I went and washed my hands with soap and water, as if I were afraid of catching something. I never could speak to her about it.

In this place where doors open and close, where slow heavy footsteps sound like a piercing echo in your ears, that star remains sewn to my heart.

Only now do I discover that I'm surrounded by my own signs.

My own yellow star. Red and yellow. Scarlet and humiliation.

With that scarlet red that inhabited Camila, with the humiliation that Tinkeleh tattooed on my skin.

Defiance and violence. Behold my dilemma.

"Damp women traveling through history and the summer," I jotted down.

From that day on I immersed myself in photos, stories, and documents about the Holocaust. I read it all voraciously and it stimulated within me an unconditional desire for justice.

A space for the abused and desperate.

Peronism was the ideal place in which to orient those feelings. The Peronism of passion, of mysticism, of marginalization, of prominence.

Jew and Peronist.

Peronist and Jew.

Woman, Jew, and Peronist.

A triple provocation.

The stories of concentration camps that I tried to decipher between books and whispers among family members became an undeniable obsession. All the barriers that Tinkeleh put in place with her silence made my journey inevitable.

My stubborn habit of concealing fear, pain, and tenderness trained my soul so that the revolution would have easy access.

Sometimes it's overwhelming to just perceive the disgusting aspects of this daily horror. I can barely make out if there is some kind of coherence to this tunnel I must travel through trying all the while not to listen, to feel, to look. However, I can't avoid the wounds caused by my discoveries. They mix insults of "Goddamn Jew" with "Fucking Peronist" in an effort to tear me apart piece by piece.

Peronist and Jew.

Peronist or Jew?

Jew and Peronist!

I pass my thick tongue over my lips. A pair of hands remove me from my body, in which I condense the murmuring of them all.

. . . Silent night, Holy night . . .

Oé, sin moverme, sin reírme . . .

A petén sem bem, tucu man, len yi . . .

. . . Ring around the rosy, pocket full of posies . . .

. . . Coo coo ca choo . . .

. . . Ashes, ashes, we all fall down . . .

The girl flying a kite and playing hopscotch. The girl from the neighborhood and blue bellflowers. The one who makes the wind blow in summer and then fills the air with the aroma of eucalyptus in winter. The one on the sidewalks of Corrientes and at the La Paz bar. The one at the Lorraine bookstore and Fiorentino's. The one of Camila and Evita. The silent one and the dissident one.

The one of the poets who doesn't give in. The one of Humberto Costantini with his poem, "*Eli Eli, lama sabactani*" (My God, My God, Why Hast Thou Forsaken Me). The one of Juan Gelman, who writes: "They are useless questions for this winter

/ one can't throw them into the fire to burn / they're no good for warming yourself in this country / they're no good for warming the country frozen in blood."

Jew and Peronist!, they grumble, shake, squeeze.

I run my tongue, lightly, over the cracked lips of my women.

18

Terezin, November 1942.

They pass in front of the synagogue that's just behind the houses on Pieval Street. They're going to see the teacher and they make an attempt at finding something to eat along the way. The classes have become an opportunity to feel human. There are poets, musicians, school teachers, chess players. Several of them attended the Gymnasium, or applied for admittance to the university. Many no longer have parents, siblings, or grandparents and they plead—like her—to find them somewhere. Tinkeleh herself has abandoned the plans she had when they took her from Minsk: the dream of traveling, of making art. Each time she tries to remember, her father's voice comes to her, though not his image, which is fading in her memory.

Language, mathematics, physics, the teacher and she are the thin thread that keeps Leah connected to the world. "The Terezin teachers are similar to the rabbis that my father used to tell me about," she thinks. Every so often she attends a meeting some of the teachers have for adults, but she doesn't feel comfortable there. One of the teachers is very religious, another bores her, and the last one annoyed her with his overstated love for Palestine, where according to him they were going to go some day. She envies the certainty with which he expresses himself and at the same time it exasperates her; she doesn't quite know why. Actually, Leah's parents had already told her about the land of Israel. It seems foolish to keep insisting on the topic here. It's too late to choose another destiny.

It's strange to her, almost diabolical, that the culture she had so admired and never had access to, not even in an important city like Minsk, is concentrated in a place like Terezin. Meeting Professor Liebschtein was like reaching the New World.

He had been transported there several weeks ago. Leah and other youths began seeing him regularly. He started to revive in Leah the spirit she had been letting slip away. She listens to him with admiration and sometimes she debates with him, recovering her former impassioned vehemence.

"You have an alert mind. If you ever want to make a great contribution to the sciences, you must question everything that is placed before you," Liebschtein tells her.

"However, Professor," Leah replies, "what you're saying has to do with theoretical mathematics, and I'm more interested in pursuing applied mathematics. For me, mathematics must be as human as literature or painting. I want a mathematics that puts practical intelligence to the test, but also includes the world's informal dreams."

"A humanist mathematics?" Professor Liebschtein draws a smile on his face. "All mathematics are human, it's just difficult to apply those codes on a daily basis."

"Professor, this place," she continues, "is a contradiction, a logical aberration. Where is the mathematical beauty in what is happening to us?"

"Quite to the contrary, this place teaches us to permanently question. Those who observed, warned, and drew conclusions

aren't here today. The rest of us have forgotten the thesis and
the antithesis; we didn't recognize them in time. A mathematics applied to the human being's capacity for resistance is what I
believe they are experimenting on with us. In these times I have
learned, Leah, that there is always the possibility of beauty and
logic, even when it would seem to suffer from a lack of meaning
in places like this."

She remains silent, her face tense, while the others listen with
interest. Tinkeleh is not entirely convinced by what the professor
says. These are hard times for everyone and skepticism is something that you go to bed and wake up with every day. Skepticism,
exhaustion, and uncertainty.

The classes have an added attraction. The teacher tells them
of events in Jewish history and stories that not all of them know,
since they come from religious homes where the Bible was the
only Jewish source allowed. He tells them about Jacob Frank,
who in 1775 was the leader of a very special group. When the
teacher alludes to the "special holidays" that Frank celebrated
with his followers to accelerate the arrival of the messianic
period, giggles of astonishment are heard and embarrassed looks
cross the faces of the straight-laced students from small villages.
He refers also to the Hasidim as true revolutionaries who allowed
the people to access God even when they didn't understand the
Sacred Scriptures; joy, song, and dance were a breath of fresh air
for the Judaism of that time. Incited by the teacher, two currents
of thought arise: the Frankists and the Hasidists, and the debate,
which inspired passion and strength in the group, went on for
days. Tinkeleh and Leah take the side of Frankism, to anger the
Hasidists, whose rigid morals amuse them.

Sometimes the teacher has them sit in a circle. He slowly wipes his glasses. He tells them that Rabbi Nahum once said: "If we were given the chance to hang all our sufferings on a nail and we could choose freely among them, each would ultimately take back his own, finding that the others were even worse." The teacher casts his eyes over the group. Tinkeleh imagines that his cunning will remain forever imprinted on her memory.

"I need to share with you a situation that arose a few days ago," comments Professor Liebschtein one day. "News has reached me from other prison camps like this one where people are preparing to resist the transfers. Like me, you probably assume that the trains are not there to take us to a better life." He looks at each one inquisitively. "I've been with an emissary from the Warsaw ghetto. He explained that they are preparing to stand up to the Germans. I won't go into detail with you, but I want us to consider together if such action is possible here. They also need to know if they can count on Terezin, because the idea is to act at several camps. In some, simultaneously, in others, whenever they are ready."

As the professor speaks, the tone of his voice becomes more serious. He asks them to think it over. They will meet again in two days to discuss it.

Tinkeleh and Leah look at one another. In one girl hope shines brightly. The other, eyes opaque, is absorbed once again in her interior monologue.

19

Terezin, May 1943.

It's been half a century
since anyone played this piano.
Its sounds as sweet
as it must have sounded then:
the gentleman's furrowed brow was like a cloud
before it rains.

Even the hinges
forgot to creak.
It's been half a century since anyone played this piano.

Our good friend, time,
emptied like a sphere without a clock, like a bee
that lived a long life
making so much honey
that it then wasted away, and let the sun turn it to ash.

Behind tightly closed eyes there is always another
seated man.
behind tightly closed eyes the keys tremble,

gently, like blood flowing from veins
when you kiss them with a knife and place upon them
a song.

Yesterday a man cut open his veins,
bribed all the birds
to sing him a melody, to sing him a melody.

Bent forward, foretelling death, you are like
Beethoven,
with a furrowed brow like a cloud before it rains.

She finds these lines on a crumpled scrap of paper upon exiting
the church. It isn't signed, but she recognizes, in the final verses,
the words of David, a boy who listened enthralled as Gideon
Klein played. She smoothes out the paper tenderly and tucks it
close to her chest. She's going to read it to Pavel and Alena when
they meet this afternoon.

The verses stay with her, like the concert that she heard in the
foyer of the old school, because it was in that room that the first
group of kids met with a teacher, and they were transported a few
days after arriving. Though Beethoven doesn't usually move her
much and even seems pretentious, in this place it startles her, a
shock that provides her with strength.

Oh, how Gideon Klein can play the piano! With a passion that
he doesn't show when he's away from the music. Actually, Tinkeleh thinks that the music doesn't distance itself it from him but
that he can't hold on to it in his daily life. Gideon is extremely
thin, and only his firm hands grant him a sense of harmony. He

had played in Prague, Vienna, and Paris, but he never speaks of it. It's only in front of the piano that his skin takes on color indicating that his blood still circulates.

David reminds her of Menachem and his countenance penetrates her like a knife to the chest. She knows it's necessary to treasure everything from the past, but at times it's crucial to rid yourself of those treasures in order to keep from falling into darkness.

She sometimes tries to remember with Leah the narrow streets of her village filled with the aromas of Friday afternoons, and all was alive with the bustle of shopping and the joy of welcoming the Sabbath. She even tries to hope that maybe her parents were able to escape to Palestine and they're going to try and rescue her from this place. Leah looks at her and in her eyes she thinks she sees a spark of other times, but it's nothing more than a fleeting illusion.

"You are like Beethoven, / with a furrowed brow like a cloud before it rains."

20

Terezin, October 1943.

Premeditated misery joins forces with illness and hunger. The Nazi leaders no longer come to visit the art school, nor do they concern themselves with keeping things clean, or organizing events for the SS tour groups. Only the new non-commissioned officers exercise any sort of command in the streets. They mistreat, persecute, create misery, and command a constant ghostly movement.

Not even work in the carpentry shop can guarantee rations of bread and hot soup. Some of the young people are terribly emaciated, and there are days when others who Tinkeleh had been with or run across the afternoon before simply disappear on the trains that "transport" once a week. The Camp orchestras continue to gather to play, at times with different musicians or without the participation of a given instrument.

Just as the transports keep taking people away, trains also arrive bringing people from new places in Europe. One can tell by the clothes they wear or the bundles they carry whether they are from villages, small towns, or big cities. Some women sport elegant hats, fur coats, and leather suitcases. The Orthodox Jews stand out with their phylacteries and long black coats, like the teachers in their immaculate suits, and the musicians gripping their instruments more tightly than their bundle of clothing.

Upon descending from the train, they all have the same look of fear and astonishment on their faces.

Sometimes she sits in a corner and tries to sketch the faces— she cares more about them here than landscapes, and besides who is going to censure her here?—of the diverse multitude that will appear like this for only the first few hours. The dispossession of belongings is carried out so quickly that within a few days no one can tell a cobbler from a scientist. She tries to capture in her drawing a glimpse of the world, a small hostile world reflected on dismal faces, skeletal shadows. Her parents wouldn't mind that she draws human figures, but those she observes aren't human. Her still lifes are of bread crumbs, tin plates, and flies. She has only a few colors left and a black pencil that she guards with her life.

Leah has dropped a lot of weight. Her delightful sense of humor and her braids as black as her eyes have lost their shine. In the carpentry shop she laboriously saws the planks of wood assigned to her, absentmindedly staring at the sawdust sparkling in a ray of light that streams through the broken window. Hours on end without speaking. She tries to help her without the guards noticing, but it's not easy doing her work and Leah's because she's weak too. They hardly speak at all. There's no desire and they must conserve energy.

During the short, meager lunch, she tries to lift her spirits with a poem she remembers, the color of the leaves in the woods, the afternoons in Minsk alive with the sounds of birds singing. "Where's Minsk?" Leah asks, dazed.

She makes an attempt at a math logic game that she learned, with some difficulty, from Leah herself. When she tells her sto-

ries about the Rabbi of Mezeritch, Leah nods and every so often
like an automaton repeats disjointed sentences about the train
that brought them to Terezin, the one they had planned to take,
and the final destination where no one is waiting.

"There's no need to speak of the future," Tinkeleh whispers.
Everyone in the Camp knows that the only thing real is the present, this day, this moment.

"That's why it's important to write, to paint, to play," the
teacher insists. "All that remains, to the delight of memory, is the
perfection of Michelangelo, the dreams of Pythagoras, the figures
of Giotto, a poem by Schiller, the words of the prophet Ezequiel.
It's the retina of the centuries," and he seems to gaze into a far
off place as he names them.

"Wars are also the retina of the centuries," says Leah in a
quiet voice, and then she sinks again into silence.

The group of youths that had started with Liebschtein is no
longer the same. Some disappear and others join in. Some excel-
lent chess players have arrived from Russia and Hungary. They
don't make a lot of effort to understand one another, because
they know that everything is contingent: perhaps they'll be here
for a time, perhaps they'll be taken away tomorrow, who knows.

They gather poems that some had left behind, they keep the
drawings of those who couldn't take them along, they cover an
incomplete sculpture with paper and they share the fleeting hope
that someday they will get their work back or that they will be
recognized in those same works.

The trains come twice a week now. They are vacating the
Camp. They say that Terezin doesn't offer the guarantee of secu-
rity.

Fight? Tinkeleh observes that the young people show little interest in it. She also doesn't know the best path to follow, but she wants to be up to date on what's going on in other places.

The teacher, who's been gathering information from the outside, tells them to spread the word that the motto is: LIVE WITH DIGNITY, DIE WITH DIGNITY. "Surely," he explains, "in other places they know the final destination of the transports, and also of the many people who are perishing from hunger or disease like the typhus that's wreaking havoc in the Camp.

"It's not easy," continues Liebschtein, "to organize resistance in Terezin. I've already informed our contacts.

"There are two apparently insurmountable problems: we are completely isolated with respect to Prague, and there is very little outside communication with non-Jews. In addition, the architecture of the fortress is practically impenetrable: the walls were constructed with enormous blocks of solid rock and the interior space is completely compartmentalized. The political prisoners are separated from the Jewish masses; the cells and barracks comprise a kind of labyrinth, which is under the continual watch of the SS. Besides, the fact that the majority of prisoners are in 'transit' makes the possibility of organizing stable groups of combatants difficult."

However, like the teacher, Tinkeleh feels ambivalent about the idea. The words of the teacher echo in her soul. She has read several newspapers that appear clandestinely from time to time, which she has translated by a Polish or Russian companion. Thus, she's able to follow the news in papers like *Unzer Veg*, *Paolei Sion*, or the *Biuletine del Bund*, that give her an approach to ideas that she knew very little about until now: Zionism, socialism, and the necessity of resisting oppression as a form of national Jewish pride.

She reads and discusses these ideas with her teacher. However, she is still confused about certain issues. Without the internal or external support to attempt something like an act of resistance, nor the strength to organize it, they need someone who is more impassioned and hardened than the teacher to provide them with the encouragement they need.

Today's news is disheartening. Liebschtein calls an urgent meeting.

"I want to tell you," he begins, in a subdued voice and with an expression of anguish, "that some of our own have died with dignity. Some time ago I received news from Warsaw, where our brothers resisted and fought valiantly before dying. The Warsaw ghetto has been reduced to ashes since May. Just a few weeks ago, in Vilna, young and old alike fought to the death.

"I wanted to transmit this news to you to renew our strength. We know that not all of us can wield a weapon. Perhaps our resistance will be in what we paint, write, or perform on stage or in music. It is our way of living in dignity and it will be our way of dying with dignity, should it so come to pass.

"It is not typhus, or starvation or the train that we should fear, but our own inability to resist daily, together, side by side and helping one another."

Some embrace in silence, others weep. Leah and Tinkeleh, holding hands like so many times before, look at each other without uttering a word.

"Let's compose a letter," proposes the teacher, "in the style of Terezin, with drawings, paintings, poems, and let us send it to our brothers and sisters, so that we know other eyes will be upon us and so that they don't feel alone."

The sidewalks become more deserted with each passing week. Those who remain are inhumanely free. They know they are free to come and go among the filth, the hunger, and the disease, and yet they have no desire for this to change. Tinkeleh senses that this joy of surviving as a person won't allow her to die. To be aware of that possible voyage, that possible transport that can happen from one moment to the next, again stirs her will to survive and keeps her going.

Only the haphazard nature of time in which events occur and the presence of a space occupied by concrete people manage to lessen the apocalyptic vision that reality presents to her; a reality of broken bodies in search of a fleeting, unattainable song.

She isn't able to remember how long she's been living in this place. So much time has passed that she no longer insists on anything except to leave a trace of herself behind to avoid the nightmares from becoming reality at a future date.

21

They gave me the nickname "Owl," and that was the name I adopted in the underground. A name given to a woman for whom "darkness is another sun."

I carefully remove the dark blindfold covering my eyes. My eyes burn and are oozing a thick secretion. They're infected. I keep the rag close by in case someone approaches and I have to put it back on. I've become so accustomed to this night that is not like other nights.

"How is this night different from all the rest, Papa?" I asked on nights long ago.

"Because on this night we did not escape from Egypt," I answer myself.

"On this night I am in Egypt," I assert.

Yesterday they brought in new cell mates, both men and women. Some of them are curled up on the floor pleading for water; others, slumped in a corner touch themselves like wounded animals. A strange odor surrounds their bodies.

I wish to be far away, to not see, to not understand, to not look. I approach each of them, barely wet their lips, and tell them to be strong. They cry, slobber, and wail. My advice to them is absurd.

Will Cesare Pavese whisper to them tonight, "Death will come and it will have your eyes." I made it through the tunnel to the other side and I'm alive. How can I help them through?

Night after night I make my way toward death in stages. What can I do for them? A groan at my side. I close my eyes in rage. Each time I do they burn intensely so I have no recourse but to open them again. My eyes are glued to the muck. My nipples are ill-prepared for the onslaught of so much filth.

Are these the same nipples that Ernesto used to caress?

I don't dare touch my own dirty, lacerated, skinny body. Will I resurrect in my own body or the one with the yellow star?

"Peronists? Fascists!" my father used to say, staring distrustfully at the friends I used to bring home. He no longer held the same sympathy for Peronism that he had in the past. He had fallen in love with Frondizi, violence went against his nature, and he detested the triumphant attitude he perceived in my so-called friends.

"If Evita were alive, she'd be a *montonera* guerilla," they shouted.

"Adonai Eloheinu, Adonai Echad," my father repeated on Yom Kippur, the day of atonement.

"Would she be a *montonera*?" I wonder.

"Chad Gadya, Chad Gadya . . . and God ate the lamb," my father insists like a litany.

It's true that the movie of your life flashes by in minutes, even those little things that seem unimportant, forgotten. Baby photos, voices, a song, something somebody said. I listen to the orders shouted by the guy who seems to be in charge of changing the guard twice a day. I also listen to other voices that go by every so often telling dirty jokes and laughing out loud. You can hear slamming doors and short steps, like climbing stairs. Sometimes they appear out of nowhere by surprise to check in on us. I prick up my ears. I know how long it will take them to get to the door and I automatically put my hood on.

The others in the cell don't speak. I try to give them a sip of water from a jar I found in the shower one day. The youngest woman has dry heaves. I don't ask them any questions. Why would I? This is like a transfer hole between the hall of horrors (and to think that I used to be frightened by the ghost train) and what's to come.

I'm becoming skeptical and I hate myself for it. The routine to which I've become accustomed is laid bare and it disturbs me.

Tinkeleh did more than I'm able to do. I'm the one who can't reach her. The abyss between us has triumphed.

Am I a prisoner of the Saint Petersburg white nights?

I remember that well kept place on Libertador Avenue, near the General Paz freeway. In the last days of our freedom, we were aware of that secret detention center and what they said about it. And now I'm here, in the dark cave, with a stinking bathroom and a shower with barely tepid water. So elegant on the outside, so filthy on the inside. Just like them.

Will death come and take my eyes?

Will I be the Chad Gadya lamb?

Who will free me from Egypt?

Who will they hang in my place on Purim?

Will I be able to answer these questions come next Pessach?

22

The clear, inquisitive eyes of my grandmother Hannah show me the way.

I recognize her face from old photos that my mother kept in a tattered old shoe box. Her gray hair was pulled back and high, away from her forehead, and she wore long dark dresses, a felt hat or a woven cap for the cold winter afternoons.

Tinkeleh looks nothing like her mother.

When I sat on her lap, my mother would squint her eyes more than usual and, in silence, stroke my hair.

She told me very few things about her mother: that she was an intelligent woman; that the only thing that frightened her was when the Germans took my grandfather away; that she would have liked to attend the university if women had been allowed to do so back then (although she made up for it with constant reading); that others sought her out for her advice because she knew how to lighten the hearts of people, a talent inherited from her father, the surly Rabbi of Mezeritch; that they took her away on the last truck leaving Minsk. Tinkeleh learned that long afterwards, when a survivor from the town, with whom she made the trip to Argentina, told her that someone was with her in Treblinka along with other persons from Minsk.

My mother's stories were fragmented. Sometimes she spoke

of Hannah's childhood in Mezeritch, the smell of onions, her father's harsh criticism, and then suddenly she would say something about life in Minsk; the woods, the birds, her friend Leah, whom she insisted on stating belonged to a family of well-educated Zionists. When she spoke of Terezin, she would only mention her classes with Professor Liebschtein, and caring for Leah and the resignation that destroyed her. The creativity of the group my mother belonged to was the main reason for her survival. That, and painting. Color and shape that remained imprisoned.

Tinkeleh is fairly short, with olive-colored skin and a round face. From her mother she inherited only the intense squint of her eyes and a certain discreet haughtiness that hasn't diminished over the years in spite of the air of resignation that is taking over like a chronic virus.

The photos of her in Buenos Aires show her dressed in dark, knee-length dresses with black or brown buttons, her jet-black hair cut short and neat, without makeup, a beret worn to one side and her thin lips pursed tightly in defiance.

Only here and now in this place am I able to understand some of the secrets that she keeps so tightly in her grip. In Terezin she lived moments of courage, camaraderie, and study that she wished to hold onto as the few salvageable treasures. She fears mentioning them will cause them to evaporate into thin air.

My father is a casual passenger in the new life that he made for himself in this country, and proof that he achieved a future. It makes her proud, but that feeling is mixed with guilt and fear when it comes to me, because I make her face destiny once again.

She comments that I inherited Hannah's ash blond hair, the impetus for leadership, the will to fight at all cost, and a certain vanity in my ironic answers. From her I got my short stature, an ochre tone of voice, the love of art, and secret courage. "From Rivka, your revolution," she told me one afternoon in a tone of bitter reproach.

The last few days there have been rumors of "transfers" and the word makes me shudder.

"History does not repeat itself," they told us. We read it in texts and our comrades recited it every time there was a conflict. However, I hear in that word the suggestion of threat present in my mother's broken voice, when she begged me, in her own way, to give up my political activism.

They removed the others from the cell and I haven't seen them since.

They were weak and I don't believe they can withstand it. I knew from the moment they brought them in. The fact that they are so young troubles me. They don't belong to my group, and yet they do. I used to train and give orders to people that age.

What are they planning to do with me? Strange things are happening, especially since they've been taking me out into the courtyard for a few minutes each day. In the hallway, toward that cramped space with a tiled floor onto which the midday sun beats down like lead, I hear voices coming from other places. Voices that I don't recognize as familiar, and even words that don't sound like police slang.

How many like me are there in this place? Are they all digging into their past? I know it isn't so.

Our male comrades are inspired by the women of other

revolutions and by Eva. They die for Eva, but in a more irrational way. My thing with Eva is emblematic, part of a paradise built around my women, from that genealogical tree of women and roots. Like a tango sung by Rosita Quiroga. Like the Sulamite woman anointed by Solomon. Like a chest made of sandalwood. Like the partisan beret worn in the Warsaw ghetto. Like Camila O'Gorman whirling her love about in the wind.

These women renew my hope. I'm taken every day to shower now and I've been given clean clothes. I'm no longer forced to wear the hood over my head. Even dinner was better. Or am I just fooling myself to make it seem that way? I fall asleep thinking of Ernesto.

He was no longer the same man with whom I discovered my sensuality that night at the Tom and Jerry Club. Over time it became more like a kind of brotherhood. Toward the end encounters with Ernesto became few and far between. Moving from house to house, fleeing from apartment to apartment, getting a small farm to hide out at, all turned intimacy into a something characterized more by desperation than desire.

For those comrades with children, the situation became even more difficult. Since the general threw us out of Plaza de Mayo, the internal arguments and fighting became more frequent. The same for my differences with Ernesto. He had a natural tendency to justify everything, to gloss over others' gaffes with a rhetoric he created based on alleged successes, certain progress made in the struggle, collective conviction.

It was surprising how devoted he and the others were to the words of the leaders when Perón went from being the "chief" to "Little López's slave."

They scoured over the orders, the internal memos, and the

counter orders and they discovered meaning in them that wasn't there. I, who had sunk my teeth into the texts of Sartre and Camus, didn't find anything surprising in the games of the "Old Man." However, they differentiated between the "Old Man" who was exiled as a revolutionary and the Perón who sold out to López Rega and Isabelita. Especially after what happened with the Plaza de Mayo.

For me, Peronism continues to be the line of thinking that will recover the honor and meaning of existence in an Argentina that was destroyed by the Nazi-capitalism of this century. It was not the third way advocated by our comrades that I longed for, but the only position possible for a country and a world that mercilessly condemns those who live on the margins. "Typical of a feminist intellectual," some of my comrades would say to me. For them, "feminist" was as insulting as the term "military gorilla" given to Perón.

Is the political activist speaking? Here I am walled in and still spouting those rigid speeches that I invented? Is it that I am these very words that I forged through a fairly cynical way of thinking?

There is no other way to lead the struggle. Revolutionaries have always thought this way. Always. Never. Everything.

What must Mordechai Anilevich have been like? A young man my age fighting with dignity to the death? He was able to do it, and I'll manage somehow. We will achieve something on this path. We were able to strike a blow even though they beat us back. The rest will come. At another moment in history it will come.

I must believe it or I won't be able to withstand the alternative.

Ernesto wasn't of the same opinion as the others on several matters, but he never defended me. When we were alone together, he would penetrate me forcefully, almost painfully, in order to break the spell that came over me. I let it all go when I'd become suspended in time with him, in that miracle of white light that flooded over me on some of those Sundays. They were Sundays that slowly disappeared from the week, hidden by surroundings that seemed more and more like Minsk than the heroic Crossing of the Andes that the Movement planned in order to liberate the continent of Latin America.

He came from a poor working-class family, and he was known as "Mauro," the same as I had been baptized "Owl." I showed him a world that had been unknown to him, and he helped me to find a spontaneity that I find difficult to practice. My thoughts speed by at a hundred miles an hour. I have the habit of relating to everything as if it were an event, with a before, a during, and an after.

I introduced him to Sylvia Plath, Dylan Thomas, Giuseppe Ungaretti, Constantine Cavafy, León Felipe: political activists knew little or nothing of poetry, barely anything of literature, but it was forbidden to mention Borges. Required readings included the speeches of Perón, Cooke, or the Tupamaros above all. Of course, they had high regard for Paco Urondo or Rodolfo Walsh, whom I admired as writers even if they hadn't been political activists as well. Ernesto-Mauro smiled at my critiques and advised me to keep them tucked neatly under my pillow: "Write them on little pieces of paper and tuck them safely away like the Wailing Wall."

Through me he gained access to other literature and jazz, and through him I learned to value the neighborhood, Italian cinema, the talent of Aníbal Troilo, Fiorentino's way with words, the genius of Astor Piazzolla.

We attended the folk music gatherings, however, as part of the bitter cup that political activism forced upon us. With the exception of Atahualpa Yupanqui and Mercedes Sosa, the music that our comrades tend to listen to is just horrid. I prefer the wailing of Altiplano music to the insipid lyrics of *cuecas* and *chacareras* that to me sound as stupid as Fritz and Franz jokes.

Since I carry around the voices of the Glostora Tango Club like baggage, for me, enjoying the lyrics of Manzi or Cadícamo was as enthralling as the rhythmic cadence of Bessie Smith. Our love kept time to the beat of Osvaldo Rovira, with an emotion similar to how I feel listening to Rugiero Ricci when he sings *Capricho Vasco*. One day I bought tickets for the nose-bleed section of the Teatro Colón where they were performing Verdi's *I Pagliacci* and it was one of the few times that I saw Ernesto cry. We reveled in those moments together.

The more he became transformed into Mauro and I into Owl, the more rigid the code we had to follow: avoid public places, sever our ties with family, and accept banishment as a means of survival.

For months we were nothing more than Mauro and Owl. But nicknames don't save you from reality, and reality showed us that they hauled us off as Ernesto and Rita.

❧ ❧ ❧

I wake up startled by a horrible noise.

Again the silence. Where could Ernesto be?

Ernesto, where are you?

Where are you, Rita?

Where could Rita be?

Will I withstand it or not?

Will he withstand it or not?

Behold, again, the question.

24

It's strange that I should be getting better in the midst of such squalor and filth.

I have the bitter certainty that I discovered Rita because of this imprisonment, in this suffering that I've been preparing for years as if it were rightfully mine. I've learned to see myself clearly in here.

I don't want to surreptitiously return to the past.

I force myself to concentrate on every fragment of my life. My body is abandoning me like Leah's did in her last days. I don't give in. I only try to understand, but that process is like boarding a train toward an unknown destination.

"I made you a chocolate cake," my mother said the last time I saw her.

I didn't know what to say, I found it impossible to tell her about the friends who were being swallowed up by the earth every day, the possibility that the same thing could happen to me at any time.

"It's been a long time since we've shared a *mate* together. Maybe I should have given you more *yerba mate* with milk," she said out loud with a forced smile.

How can I tell her what I needed? Words to explain what she kept hidden, words for her dark, blank stare. That stare of hundreds, of thousands, who accuse by means of what they keep silent.

I wrapped my arms tightly around her and felt her fragile body through the faded robe. A robe that she would use until it was little more than a threadbare rag.

It was there, at that moment, that she gave me a yellowed slip of paper, folded over several times and tied shut. I opened it carefully. It was a handwritten text and the last line read, "Leah."

"I've wanted to give you this for a long time. It's the last thing that my friend wrote in Terezin."

Without my mother knowing it, I placed Leah's page in the box, hidden away with the yellow star. The contents now belonged to both of us: drawings, scribblings, poems, a scrap of striped cloth, a small metal pitcher, a faded ribbon, and now Leah's page. That's where it should stay.

"The butterflies don't float in the air here either," Leah, and my tears begin to well in my eyes as if they had their own time, place, and life.

I add LEAH to the women on my wall who are all in good health.

Terezin, July 1944.

News arrived that the Germans are retreating on all fronts, which explains why there has been so little movement in the Camp, and yet the past few days she has seen unusual activity. There are a lot of prisoners working on repairing and cleaning up many of the walls and streets. They are also building some sort of stage.

While there are now but a few remaining with whom to share her doubts and hopes, she keeps a daily close watch on what's happening in the central courtyard. She consults a few people and what she finally learns strikes her as extravagant, but true. It seems that some important authorities are going to visit the Camp and they are preparing for a performance of Verdi's *Requiem*, with orchestra and choir, to mark the occasion. She can't believe it. She feels a strange happiness mixed with fear. Routine allows for a life without expectations. Anything new can bring unusual circumstances with it, and those circumstances are almost always worse.

She contacts a Mr. Schächter, the program director. Rafael Schächter is a stocky, friendly person who is completely immersed in his final and definitive obsession—to perform a Jewish Requiem that exalts the human condition over all iniquity. Tin-

DAUGHTER OF SILENCE

keleh manages, during scarce moments of free time, to get him to tell her how he's going to put together what for him will be the requiem of the triumph of life over death. He speaks in a firm voice revealing a contained passion.

The first soloist he located is Francisco. He's the son, grandson, and great-grandson of synagogue cantors, and he was one of the first to arrive in Terezin. Schächter had heard him sing in the barracks one Friday evening and he started working with him on the proper Latin pronunciation needed for the Requiem. Searching among the thousands of inhabitants, he was introduced to a soprano, a splendid young woman with a marvelous voice. Finally, he found a mezzo-soprano who knew all of Verdi's work, and with them he put together a small orchestra and choir. He lacked only a bass.

They found a basement where they can rehearse and the director tries to get his idea across to them. The Requiem is a work like no other that speaks directly of the Final Judgment, wherein murderers will be condemned by those whom they themselves condemned: slaves, the oppressed, those put to death. Ire will gash their souls, if they have any, it says.

People find out through word of mouth what Schächter is planning and musicians begin volunteering spontaneously. No one wants to miss the opportunity to stand and be counted, perhaps for the last time, in this sort of musical crusade. For some, it's the chance to reacquaint themselves with the instrument they lovingly carried instead of a coat or food. For others, it's finding again the person that they once were and believed no longer existed. Some of the policemen in the Camp secretly provide them with musical scores they were able to purchase in Prague.

The hardest task is obtaining the instruments. Some people had their instruments seized upon entering the Camp while others exchanged them for clothing or a ration of food. At any rate, they managed to gather violins, violas, trumpets, a trombone, and two cellos thanks to certain transactions with policemen and peasants, along with vendors who came into the Camp to sell food. Likewise, they salvaged some from the belongings confiscated from the Jews from other regions that the Reich sent to Terezin on trains.

Schächter got a promise from the officials to not transport any of the participants in the program nor their families, but of course the authorities don't keep their word and one day twelve orchestra musicians disappear and are replaced the next day with twelve others. The conductor's first reaction is to abandon the project, but he knows that that would cost them all their lives so he decides to proceed, turning his pain into music in an almost brutal effort. For him, combining Italian music, Latin text, and Catholic prayers with Jewish singers and musicians is a dream as strange as the place they inhabit together. It is a challenge that could have presented itself to them only here.

"The Nazis are not common murderers," says Schächter in a hoarse voice "but rather demons for whom abuse and treason are a way of life. But we shall go on, because playing well will be our cry of triumph."

On one occasion an SS officer enters in the middle of rehearsal to perform an inspection, his nightstick in hand and his boot heels clicking. They sing out loud "Hosanna! Hosanna!" ignoring his presence.

One day, without anyone knowing why, the deportations

from Terezin are halted. The choir and the orchestra are able to rehearse without interruption. Shortly thereafter, they are given a date for the concert.

A few days before the performance, soldiers burst into the Jewish hospital and empty it. They drag out people who cannot walk; there are gunshots, wounded, dead who are taken to the crematorium. Two hours of screams and chaos until they hear the order that explains the senselessness of what is going on.

The hospital is being transformed into a theater.

The top brass of Prague and the High Chiefs of Berlin, among them a man whose name some utter with horror—Adolph Eichmann, will be arriving in Terezin on Saturday morning. The ceremony will be complete with wine, meals, military decorations, and speeches.

When Eichmann learns that the Jews are preparing a performance of Verdi's Requiem for him he bursts into ferocious laughter. "How can these stupid Jews sing about their own deaths?" he says in German and loud enough so that the Jewish wait staff serving his table can hear him.

When it came time for the show, the SS and the guards locate their seats in the darkened room in front of the stage, which is the only thing that remains lit. Backstage, Tinkeleh and all those participating in the performance are brimming with excitement, as is Leah, weak and stricken with fever. Tinkeleh had to drag her friend there.

Schächter is giving the last of his stage directions while singers and musicians tune their voices and instruments.

The Requiem begins like a whisper and as it builds, the voice of the tenor sings: "Guilty now I pour my moaning. All my shame with anguish owning. Spare, o God, Thy suppliant groaning.

Worthless are my prayers and sighing, yet, good Lord, in grace complying, rescue me from fires undying." An ambience of exaltation and mixed passions follows. Fear, pride, hatred, unburdening, release, all are heard in the words of the song. Schächter, sweating and joyous in his conducting, is exalted.

The *Confutatis Maledictus* echoes in the room like a storm: "When the wicked are confounded, doomed to flames of woe unbounded. Call me, with Thy saints surrounded. Low I kneel, with heart submission, see, like ashes my contrition, help me in my last condition."

The rest follows in a stampede of sound until the *Lacrymosa* comes like a bolt of lightning streaking across the first part, but the conductor continues amidst the darkness with the jubilation of the Jews who sing "We shall not be overcome."

The recitations, the chorus chants, the ode, the violins, and the cello lead up to that voice that causes all to tremor in the end with the soprano's voice as she cries: "Libera Me!" She's accompanied by the message of the chorus "Deliver us!" "Freedom!" blares the orchestra. "Freedom!" echo the timpani and with the final "Libera Me," the curtain falls.

Following a dense silence, Eichmann can only applaud. The rest then join in the applause.

Schächter and his musicians, drenched in sweat, receive a standing ovation. They are no longer concerned with what may happen. The only thing that matters is that they now know that they haven't lost the human strength that upheld them through iniquity and glory for five thousand years. They belong to the people that shall not perish.

Toward the end of the summer the order comes for all those who participated in the performance to be transported. It is a day of intense pain in Terezin. Good-byes here are rendered meaning-less. Some leave their instruments behind with a friend, others carry them along like when they arrived, and there are those who leave them at the hospital where they performed the Requiem, like a token offering to what they were, which remained forever in that place.

26

Terezin, July 1944.

In spite of losing her teacher, her friends, and her strength and in spite of the typhus that is feverishly consuming her, Leah seems to regain her determination one morning. She begins to write anxiously in her cramped hand a text that she offers to Tinkeleh saying, "So that something of me might survive." Tinkeleh reads it over and over and keeps it among her most precious of belongings.

> There are no butterflies here. No, here the butterflies don't float in the air.
>
> Only silence is heard in the Camp, while in some other place, in an old school, Gideon Klein strokes his instrument and leans against it as he relives lost dreams.
>
> Another adolescent like me, a passionate poet, a rebellious youth from Prague, remembers his home town, so far away, so old, so vital.
>
> There are no butterflies here. No, here the butterflies don't float in the air, Pavel Fridman, because this is the Camp and butterflies have always sensed the smell of death, because their lives are short and only the flowers hold dreams in their petals.
>
> Sitting on some street curb, engrossed in thought, the murmur

of a far off and frightening life reaches me like the grass that grows in the Camp: clandestine and dry.

Men and women tear light from their impassioned song in a Requiem of music and pain meant to turn our hell into a twilight rain shower.

There are no butterflies here. No, they don't float in the air here because they avoid the pathways in the Camp.

Sing, Jews, while you remember Vienna, Munich, Minsk. Sing and spew forth the words to "Libera Me" in your hearts today, so as to attract the butterflies to fly over the Camp.

The timpani accompany them in their flight while I hear: "I shall multiply your seed like the sands of the earth. I shall bless those who bless you and curse those who curse you."

Yes, there will be butterflies in Terezin today: Pavel, Alena, Eva, Franta, Liebschtein, Schächter, who loved us, painted us, and sang our life.

Schächter marked out the meter for the "Recordare," and I engrave on my forehead "Re-cor-dar-e," Remember, so that the strange road that led us here will be made known, here on earth as it is in heaven. There where the butterflies float on the breeze.

Tinkeleh folds the paper and puts it in her pocket, believing it will someday be the legacy she leaves for a daughter.

27

Terezin, November 5, 1944.

The puppet theater is no longer operating and no one goes to work at the carpentry shop. No one has the strength to continue. The soup lines are constantly filled with people waiting for a portion of hot water and potato peel soup. Endless waiting to sometimes get nothing more than a piece of stale bread, or scraps of something floating in the water.

The SS march by in military formation and they are seen in groups on all the streets. Insurrections in other camps keep them on the alert. Ever since they hauled off everyone who performed Verdi's Requiem, neither the children's theater or the orchestra is performing. Friends and acquaintances are vanishing and the one-time busy, noisy streets of the Camp are falling silent. Nevertheless, there remain a goodly number of people.

"Terezin is a place where adults and children can live like in freedom." Tinkeleh read this on a street sign. The hurtful impact of the word "like" jumps out at her. They are "like" human beings, "like" workers, "like" children, "like" slaves.

She thinks of Leah, shattered by typhus, watching feebly as the teacher and his pupils are shoved onto the train. That day it had taken her nearly half an hour to convince Leah to go to class with her in spite of the fever. She finally did, but they arrived late and that saved their life.

The loss of their teacher fills her with hatred but at the same time gives her the drive to keep fighting for the both of them, to not turn into a ghost of herself. But every incident that bolsters her also destroys Leah.

She dashes to the teacher's house to try and rescue notebooks, notes, drawings, loose papers, and all that her classmates couldn't gather up in the haste of being expelled from the building. She collects it all and piles it in a corner she hopes is safe and not easy to find. She reaches into her pocket and pulls out two sheets of paper with poems written by her friends and begins to draw on them. Sitting on her wooden bench that she still has among her few belongings she begins to sing "*Schwartze oign, schwartze tzeplaj,*" in the same tune she remembered from the sister of the woman in Minsk who held her son tightly and faced the firing squad.

She draws with hatred, with tenderness, with pain on the paper with the poems she found. She draws and sings, hums and paints, in anger, in frustration, in desperation:

I

Terezin has turned lovely
before the gazes of all
and on the streets you can hear
the footsteps of the passersby.

That's how I see
the Terezin Camp,

this square kilometer of space
apart from the world.

II

Oh, how death grips the earth
trapping one and all;
even those who always go about with a
stiff upper lip, and noses in the air.

But justice will reign
over the world
and the lips of the poor
shall taste sweetness again.

She reads "Miroslav Kosek," that twelve-year-old boy with
deep black eyes.

The Garden

The garden is small
and smells of roses.
Along the narrow path
a boy wanders by,
Tiny, small, lovely,
like a blossoming bud.
When the bud perishes
the boy will no longer exist.

"Franta Bass," who with her seventeen silent years asked anxious
questions when Professor Liebschtein's class would meet.

Seated on the little bench, with her bag ready, she's next to

Leah when the SS come looking for them with guns pointed at their heads.

She carries that little cloth bag that she's kept with her since leaving home, to which she adds a scrap of bread that she got from a friend in the kitchen and the bottle of water that the teacher had suggested they have ready, her only change of underwear that's tattered but clean, the poems with the sketches and the letter. She's also carrying her handmade wooden bench, which is ripped from her hands as she's shoved onto the car of a very long train. She sees that there are several trains waiting and that thousands of people are being loaded onto them. She would never have imagined that so many were still living in Terezin, especially since the transports had been occurring more frequently. She tries to settle into a spot inside the car near the door where it's easier to breathe. When they snatched the bench from her they took all that remained of her home, what little remained of Minsk. She was able to rescue Leah from the hospital and practically carried her, with the help of others, to the train. Next to her, Leah takes on the appearance of a yellow, fever-racked twig covered with skin. The acrid air and foul smell of so many bodies crammed together is joined by the moaning of women, the murmur of young people who haven't lost the energy to fuss, and the frightened voices of the few remaining children who tremble and cling to their mothers.

The train advances at high speed and she tries to peek through a crack in the door to see the passing fields. She had dreamt of them in greens, earth tones, blues and now that she sees the fleeting landscape passing before her eyes they seem more beautiful and luminous than she remembered.

She clutches the bag containing the small treasures of her life close to her chest. She slumps down leaning her back against that of another person, as she stares at Leah who's curled into a shapeless lump.

Her breathing is slow and scarcely audible. Maybe at the end of the trip there will be a river waiting for her. What color will the river be? Oh, she'd like that! To bathe in a river like the one her mother told her about where she grew up near Mezeritch, or like the rivers in Germany, like the ones the girl who played the flute in Schächter's orchestra spoke of so lovingly. The Germany adored by the young girl, and for which her grandfather and father had fought, now considered her to be a pestilence that must be eradicated.

She thinks that the Jewish Germans have a far lesser understanding of what's happening to them than the Russians or Poles, who are more familiar with pogroms and persecution. As a consequence, they are less shocked than the Germans and Viennese, whose Judaism, even amidst so much misery, seemed strange and even removed from their own. Every so often she takes a sip of water, wets Leah's lips, and wipes the cold sweat from her face.

"Maybe there will be a river for us to bathe in," Tinkeleh whispers into her ear, hardly able to tell that she's breathing.

28

I set the tin plate to one side. I stand up and attempt to stretch my legs. My eyes are burning quite a lot. Someone came a few days ago and applied an ointment that stopped the infection, but the sharp pain still stabs at me.

"Keep your eyes closed when you remove the blindfold. It will help them to heal faster," I heard a neutral voice tell me. It sounded pleasant among so much noise and absence. Since then I've stopped using the black rag.

Once again the night. I delve into what I refuse to forget. In this untilled field of absences that I cultivate, there is still a small space where I find myself; when I untie myself, describe myself, discover myself, become muddled in myself.

I never had a friend like my mother's Leah. The girls in my neighborhood were strangers to the kind of disquieting concerns that troubled me. In high school I had occasional friends with whom I shared intercollegiate basketball games. Haydée was a circumstance, Elena a possibility. I found both of them disconcerting and I fled from them both. I discovered sports at that age on my own because my parents never sent me to an athletic club. Sending me to a Jewish school was enough for my parents. I joined the Ken Zionist Club on my own. I was encouraged by my father's Zionism but it was against the wishes of my mother who told me "Don't even think of making *aliyah*," in other words, going to live in Israel. So many things we had in common and how little she knew me.

In this "sunken Navy submarine," in this hell hole, I realize that I never went to kindergarten. Was I like Tinkeleh's wooden bench to my parents?

Or did I build a world in the image and likeness of her fears?

Did I choose violence in order to place limits on her secrets?

I wring the words until they are all dried out.

For now I am nothing more than a plate of food, a shower, a few minutes of sun, longings, muted regrets, questions, hundreds of disturbing questions, doubts that I grew up with and turned into certainties. We both live within me and through me. I tear Tinkeleh and myself from my heart so that these monsters get nothing from me.

The promised land doesn't exist, I say.

I tried to cross the wilderness without waiting forty years and the sand swallowed me up.

29

It must be Christmas. There are fewer guards and this morning they handed out slices of pannetone. Christmas at the Navy School of Mechanics. This revolutionary, Jewish *Yiddishe meidele* eating pannetone in a clandestine Navy prison! Who would have imagined.

However, on this night that is not like other nights nothing is as real as these walls and this tile floor. I feel closer to Tinkeleh tonight than to myself, closer to that resigned, wooden Christ than to King David. I would like to have the courage of Jesus to resurrect and recite the Psalms, out loud, for my women.

I am not made solely of what remains of me. I'm not delirious. "Silent night, Holy night . . ." I want to toast, eat nougat, give Ernesto a hug with the glance of an eye, caress my mother's secrets, my father's stories, accept this undeniable desolation that carries on among so many ghosts. I sought to imitate Judith, but I failed to cut off Holofernes's head. The military training wasn't enough; what's more, shredding the past is part of our defeat and fleeing from what we are, a danger that costs us our soul. I understood the flimsy rules of resistance to which they clung, because I also vacillated between courage and excitement. The difference is that I was moved by the mysteries of a history that I believe in, and they by the conviction of building a miraculous future.

❦ ❦ ❦

I hear the sound of empty bottles against the floor and I smile. I remember conversations with friends talking about love, family, children, the values and concepts they said they were fighting for and that they defined with a confidence that left me speechless. It was like a survey that they all answered in unison:

Love = The poor

Family = Create your own without looking back

Children = Many, for the revolution

Values = All for the people

Ernesto believed in those concepts and sometimes I was temporarily caught up in his enthusiasm.

When memories manage to filter through the wounds, I survive.

The emphasis they used to place on a uniform happiness made me laugh at them more than admire them. If the struggle wasn't an effort to feel differently, then what was the point? We got into insignificant arguments in which duty, logic, and ideas were amalgamated into a single word: Struggle! The rest would follow. That's why I avoided discussing such topics with my comrades. Only with Ernesto, curled up on the mattress in some temporary hideout where we would spend the night, did I confess my troubles without feeling suspicious stares upon me.

He told me of his postponed plans to become an airplane mechanic. He would burst into laughter and say: "I'm going to alter the destination of the damned oligarchs. I'll put them all on a fighter-bomber and they'll be on their fucking way." He stared at me knowing full well that it annoyed me. Those kinds of statements seemed ridiculous: "The Sheraton Hotel Children's Hospital," "Neither Yankees or Marxists, but Peronists." It was like saying "we have the best meat in the world," and other preposterous statements that undermined convictions and appealed to the slogans used by the enemy, except with a revolutionary's decalogue. It was as lineal and imbecilic as those against which we were fighting.

Such declarations from Ernesto made me quiver. They sounded too much like the Nazi phrase, *Deutschland über alles*— Germany above all—I'd say to him, acting like I was angry and caressing his dark, wet hair. I insisted such statements were loathsome since they masked the inability for clear thinking. He tried to convince me, with a gentle touch, that they were only jokes meant to "rile this persecuted Jewish girl." The truth was he didn't want to argue with me. We had precious little time together. They were closing in on us.

I hear footsteps. I count them, but there's no need to guess. It's the fat man who takes the swing shift watch. He's one of the few who doesn't strike fear into you. He offers me a glass of cider, clinks his bottle against it and says, looking in the other direction, as if lost in a drunken stupor that makes up for having to spend New Year's Eve in this dump:

"Cheers! Happy New Year, baby doll!"

It's been so long since I've tasted anything sweet that it makes me gag. The fat man takes my reflex as an insult and between belches and guffaws he turns around and shouts: "Fuck you. It's your loss," and he locks the door behind him.

I remember Christmases when I was little. The neighbors

would celebrate with gifts, Christmas trees, sparklers and fireworks, and I would secretly create a manger—with baby Jesus and all—out of empty Tomasito string boxes, grass I'd picked in the nearby Plaza Los Andes, and lead soldiers posing as the three wise men.

I still get a laugh from the look on my parents' faces when they discovered what I had been up to. They didn't know whether to scold me or laugh, so they began to explain to me once again the difference between Catholics and Jews. That episode changed something in them, because every sixth of January from then on I received a gift for Three Kings Day. I tried to convince them over the years of how nice it was to celebrate what we liked from both religions, but I never managed to discuss it without them getting mad. Living in a Catholic country is one thing, my father would say, but assimilating their customs and practices is another. My mother would get angry saying; You're turning into a *shiksa*, a convert. It's those friends of yours that fill your head with nonsense.

I look at the glass of warm cider in this cramped little room. A while back they hauled off several people from the adjoining cells, the same way they'd brought them in: suddenly and violently.

What should I ask for the sixth of January?

This is almost like a manger, but without straw.

The three wise men are missing to show me the way back home.

I want to go home. I didn't leave bread crumbs behind like Hansel and Gretel, but I know the way. If not, the wicked old witch is going to toss me into her oven. Oven. It stabs me like a knife. *Arbeit Macht Frei*. Crematorium. They told me history does not repeat itself. Who can guarantee that I won't end up in the fire?

My dark sense of humor terrifies me. I touch my body that now weighs twenty pounds less and I feel Ernesto's hands running over each rib, each hip bone. I'm hurt and I hurt mercilessly. Over and over with the word games in this head that never stops thinking. Nothing but memories. Nothing but literature.

I try to switch it off, but I am what I am, like in the tango. Like Margot or Madame Pinzón. I didn't banish them. They still sing along with me. Like warm milk without *yerba mate* that slightly nauseates you. Like a knitted scarf that's wider than it is long to protect me.

Tinkeleh approves. She scratches my head and picks out the nits that multiply like life itself.

Queen bee, I tell myself. Slave to your silence, I tell myself. Open ending? I ask myself.

30

After several days of silence there's suddenly a lot of commotion. The usual fat guy comments that I'm to start work. It's what some comrades do when they are transferred out of the main area. I see them in the bathroom and we eye each other up and down. They don't seem willing to open their mouths. Those who work on the outside seem more put together and better fed. Rumor has it that they are working on a special "job" for the Admiral, whom everyone here on the inside refers to in admiration and fear.

It's odd that you no longer hear the gut-wrenching screams. I also don't see anyone crumpled on the floor of open cells that I would catch of glimpse of as they take me to shower. Not even any moans and groans to keep my own pain company.

At noon we have lunch in what looks like an open barracks with tiled floors. Esther is there, along with others whose names I don't know but recognize. They seem to be the ones who work here. They speak very little, only what's necessary, and in hushed tones. However, Esther, who was always looked up to in the struggle, seems to be coping very well. She's the one who knows by heart the writings of General Perón, the books by Cooke, and everything published in Latin America on the revolution and guerrilla warfare. Is she brilliantly laying out a plan to fool them?

Counting the little noodles in the soup is an entertaining way to pass the time. There are exactly eighty-six, seven less than the other day and twenty-five more than the day before yesterday. In addition, they feed us fresh bread. It's New Year's day.

I look carefully at the colored noodles. Seeing colors changes my mood. I realize that darkness has been a constant companion and I, like a blind woman, tried during this time to hold onto images and past times that today seem far off in the distance.

I have to find the right moment to ask Esther what the hell this is all about.

It's not the darkness of night in which I live that detaches me from colors, but the emptiness into which I'm sinking and the shadow that covers and chokes off everything.

Esther was one of the most involved in the movement who volunteered for all kinds of tasks:

Planned assault: yes, planned assault.

Throw a bomb: yes, throw a bomb.

Picket a strike: yes, picket a strike.

I shared a few minor jobs with her. She inspired confidence and had an esprit de corps about her. I perceived that something was different about her. Her stare. Did my own not change? Her limpid eyes reflected fleeting shadows. Had my own not become furtive? Furtive but loyal, I thought.

Nerval's *Epitaph* reads: "He wanted to know it all / and he attained nothing."

Yes, I want to know it all, everything that I was denied from knowing, everything that they kept from us.

Auschwitz, November 1944.

Upon descending the train she sees only a giant stone arch with the inscription: *Arbeit Macht Frei.*

The irony of it makes her shutter. *Arbeit Macht Frei,* work shall set you free, she repeats under her breath.

Leah stays in the train car with a good many other traveling companions whose voyage has come to an end. She doesn't get the chance to tell her good-bye before Leah is yelled at, beaten with a club, and shoved into a long line of women who are forced to strip naked. She and other young women are lined up but not ordered to undress. She holds her small bag tightly.

Shivering in the cold, damp barracks she is nothing but a ghost with a shaved head and coarse striped uniform. She perceives the smell of thousands of women who are already gone and she repeats under her breath, *Arbeit Macht Frei.* It occurs to her that all that she lost during these years is condensed right here, all the horror she imagines in the sinister landscape being portrayed before her very eyes.

Alone and curled into a ball on the tiles while outside night has fallen and all is calm. I get close to that neighborhood girl that I strived to sweep under the rug, with the same moldy broom that matches Tinkeleh's faded robe.

Felipe goes by, on his usual pass, and Esther too who winks at me and sends me strange signals, something like: "It's okay, it will soon be your turn." Lately they seem happy and they even talk amongst themselves without taking precautions.

Ernesto, where are you?

I reel from the pain of not knowing and my stomach knots up when I think of him. That air of political activist who truly loves what he does. I knew several who were better at it, but few who were as sensitive.

Ernesto, those arms to wrap myself in, those legs around my waist. I need love, not silence. I say it in front of this mirror wall that undresses me. The warmth of hands, without reservations. Devour my women. They devour me.

Is it too late?

All that I was drawn to has disappeared. However, that dark passion that I'm afraid to name, the same as hers, is what I need to rescue so that I don't turn into a pillar of salt.

I must push forward. Will I be able to leave her behind?

Now that I have access to such simple things as pencil and paper, I write. Words that might remain beyond the wall. Closer to her, to your *"liulinke main meidele,"* to share together a few sips of *yerba mate* with milk. I need to put on weight, though you may not believe it. I'm very skinny, as thin as your ghosts. I've become one of them. I come from them, the ocean could not drown them.

33

I'm tired of crying. The tears spring forth and leave me empty inside this cell. I'm slowly losing the notion of time. Every instant is a fraction absorbed by an eternal day. Images emerge and the silence protects them.

In the past months the daytime and nighttime sounds have changed. There are fewer prisoners and less vigilance. Where are they taking them?

I toss and turn. I make an effort to remember pleasant sensations. I concentrate on the smell of coffee coming from the Bar Colombia on Corrientes and Talcahuano. That unmistakable aroma floats in the air on every corner along Corrientes.

I think about that morning two years ago when together with the comrades we listened to a recording of one of the "Old Man's" speeches. Perón indeed spoke to them. He gave them the strength to keep up the struggle. He was a leader, protector, counselor. He was a politician and a strategist who was among the very best, they said.

When the recording ended, the comrades spent hours discussing the meaning of every sentence he'd spoken.

I didn't consider myself a fanatic like Ernesto, Manolo, and Esther were. There were things that I didn't share with my comrades; for example, they censured certain literature or the world of rock music. I believed these to be cultural limitations rather than political mistakes, especially on the part of some comrades who showed a particular disdain for culture. I didn't care. I wasn't fighting solely so that everyone could eat, I'd reply. They mistrusted my ideals, but not my loyalty. I detested their certainty but I admired their enthusiasm.

Was I a member of the petit-bourgeois, as Manolo told me one afternoon when he'd become particularly annoying? "Could be," I answered him, "but with more brains than you when it comes to thinking objectively." I was a militant and a Peronist.

They consider me a tolerable Jew. Why do I put it like that? Is it my mother that once again places herself between others and myself? Unlike others I know in the Movement, I've never denied my Jewish condition. And I've never said anything as stupid as: "I'm of Jewish origin."

Although my behavior is something of a rarity for them, they tolerate it because I've got guts, I'm a hard worker, and I'm creative.

What the fuck good is responsibility doing me now?

My throat is sore. It's often hard to remember now! Not the whole picture, but the particulars that make me who I am and not who they want me to be.

Not listening to conversations for months on end makes one forget the meaning of words. Talking to yourself limits your vocabulary. It's as if words belonged to another galaxy. Sometimes I imagine them floating in the space above the room, like when I was little and had a fever. Huge, weightless words. Stars. Sponges. My parents trying to ease my pain with hot tea and lemon and a nice sweet fig at the bottom of the glass. She's got her warm milk before bed, and he's got tea and herbal drops.

One of the most unbearable things in here is the cold.

I'd love to have something hot to see if it eases the pain. The guards seem a bit more attentive, which makes me feel uneasy, although a little more comfortable, like when I asked them to bring a blanket and a pad to lie on. When he brought the blanket, the fat man with the cider also brought me a cigarette "so that later you don't say bad things about me," and he lit it for me. Such an act of kindness is a bad sign.

I inhale deeply, even though it's dark tobacco and unfiltered.

Have a smoke and sing a tango, "It's night out and the rain's pouring down."

That story that repeats itself, with the same rain but without that terrible thirst for adventure. I smile and sing:

> Come to me, old friend
> you said as you toasted me
> with your glass of fine champagne.
> The story repeats itself
> My sweet blond young thing.

A crystal glass, bubbling champagne, and me dolled-up like a showgirl. I burst into laughter like a madwoman.

The parody I am gives me a chuckle. The first moment of happiness in a long time that solely clings to the fact of being alive, singing, better fed, and with a job to perform in the archives of the Navy School of Mechanics.

Pure fiction, I say out loud. Pure fiction, girl. And not even French, English, medieval, or contemporary.

The comrades would sure get a kick out it.

Yes, my life has been spent ruminating words passed from mouth to mouth, chewed up, shredded pulp.

I am a speech. I discover I'm like a cassette that traces a face, a body, and a reinforced soul. The silence has silenced me. I surrendered to your silence. I melted into her silence. "Be a woman like the grass." Did I do it? Here in this compulsory and filthy spiritual retreat. What irony! What a brutal way to suffocate! To realize that I am only words, only vain words. I who love words so, to learn that I cannot be more than what I describe. Whatever I feel will remain in Leah, Rivka, Haydée, and the others.

"Pure fiction!" I shout again. Pure fiction, girl.

Buenos Aires, August 1946.

They went to pick her up at the Hotel for Immigrants, which was more of a way station than a hotel.

Her cousin Surele, who's now called Sarita and who married cousin José, lived in a tenement house on Chiclana Street, two blocks from La Plata Avenue. Shortly thereafter she found out that the house is near a place where they play soccer called "the field" (*el campo*). She learns this from her nephew Ariel, who's a soccer fanatic and tells her all the time about San Lorenzo, a team whose players might as well be members of the family. He names them one by one with a lot of passion so that she can memorize them. Memory is exactly what she doesn't want to have.

Her head is filled with other things, so many things since she boarded the ship in Marseilles and arrived in Buenos Aires. Everything is mixed up in her. So she remains silent. The silence makes her cousins, nieces, and nephews impatient with her.

For Tinkeleh, this cousin she barely knows is as much a stranger as the neighbors who greet her with affection, or her brother-in-law, that is to say her cousin from Mezeritch. Mezeritch and Minsk are such far off names that she dare not pronounce them out loud.

It all happened too quickly. She spent almost no time at all in the Hotel for Immigrants, and suddenly she finds herself living in a neighborhood of a strange city, where they speak a language that's difficult to pronounce. She tries sometimes to say good morning, good afternoon, how are you, so that she doesn't come across as unfriendly, but for now she can't go beyond polite exchanges.

Surele is quite a bit older than Tinkeleh. She arrived in Buenos Aires with her cousin-husband twelve years ago, in spite of the opposition of her father who dearly loved his first-born daughter, but with the approval of her mother, an open-minded, intelligent woman who believed that the Jews wouldn't have much of a future in Europe, a land that had always been hostile to them.

When she departed, they gave her a goose down bedcover made by her father. Her mother embroidered a monogram of her initials onto a white linen cloth that she purchased in the village market, the best she could find, and the only lasting thing she could pass on to her.

Surele's parents were Orthodox Jews from a small village. They kept themselves occupied with household chores and upholding the precepts of the Torah. However, when her mother had the chance, she liked to read, converse with people who could tell her news from the world outside they knew little about, but upon which they depended for their sustenance. If she were able she would travel to a bigger town on any excuse she could find. Her husband loved her and as long as she didn't go against any religious precept, he let her do as she pleased.

That's why, even though her father disapproved, Surele's

mother sent her to the home of the Rabbi of Mezeritch, Tin-keleh's grandfather, to continue her education in an important town instead of in the village where they lived.

When she reached the age to enroll in courses in Minsk, for which she would move into Tinkeleh's home, she met José and they were pressured by her mother to marry and go to America to try their luck in the name of the whole family.

Some dreamed of leaving behind poverty and persecution. Hannah had supported the initiative believing that they would meet again someday, because the world wasn't only made up of small towns, like the majority of ignorant Jews she knew assumed, each town the same as the next and where everyone led the exact same life, and lived in the same state of boredom.

She remembers Surele's letters that her parents would read out loud and that arrived farther apart each time. She also recalled her comments about a noisy city, very different but exciting, and their efforts to adapt.

The stories get mixed up with her own. Her arrival in Buenos Aires, the first day of work in the shirt factory a few blocks from her cousins' house. They employ other immigrant women like her there: Italians, Spaniards, or Poles with whom she almost never exchanges a word during the exhausting work shifts. It's a Babel of faces and languages.

Within a few months she began to learn about things that she never imagined even existed, others she had forgotten, and many more that she no longer wished to remember. Among them the liberation of Auschwitz, the hospital, the ship, the search to find other members of her family, Surele's letter, and the passage to Buenos Aires. The world had become so small over the last few years that she needed to rediscover sounds, words, objects that for her had ceased to exist. She flees, without realizing it at times, from anything that might seem like affection.

Not even Sarita and José get anything from her beyond a sense of gratitude. Only with her nephews does she allow herself gestures that seem to float up from some moment in her life that she can't pinpoint.

She submerges herself in her daily work until she's exhausted. When she returns from the factory she helps Sarita with the meals, the ironing, and preparing lunches for the next day.

Early in the morning she crosses the large patio that all the tenements open onto. She does so before the other women occupy the wash tubs and she drinks a few *mates*, a habit that calms her, and that gradually replaces her tea with lemon. *Mate* is companionship and solitude at the same time. Tinkeleh doesn't need anyone else to drink it with and she makes it her inseparable companion, silent and faithful.

The cold has no effect on her. The climate of Buenos Aires is very mild compared to what she has known. Even during what they call winter here it doesn't snow.

Some Saturday evenings her cousins get together with friends, fellow shipmates or people from their hometown and they play twenty-one with poker cards while she listens to them laugh and talk, lying on the sofa, trying to read a few newspapers in order to learn the language.

Is this what her mother wanted for her? But she's alive and her mother's not. She wraps herself in Surele's down comforter. The laughter she hears hurts. They have the right to have fun because they didn't come back from hell. She on the other hand has to hide the horror that the cheerfulness of others causes her. The profound fissure in her soul when she finds herself smiling with a workmate at the factory.

You survived, Tinkeleh! She repeats. You survived! And she covers her head in pride and rage.

35

Buenos Aires, December 1947.

She seldom draws. Not only because she has very little time to do so, but also because she's a different person from who she once was. The things she loved, her illusions of becoming an artist, her friends from Terezin, who still live on in her dreams, are only painful reminders of the past.

She loathes the night because it torments her. She submerges herself in it like it was a cold, deep lake that takes her breath away. At night she returns to those nights where no one owned the following day.

She loves the light, open spaces, and the rain. She enjoys painting instead of drawing like before. The color fills spaces that smell of the forest, of firewood, of people with names and not numbers. In order to draw again she'd have to remember it all, and she's not willing to do that. She makes an effort to be part of this new world that's so different and that helps her to forget who and where she was. Painting, on the other hand, is a salutary experience that enables her to hide shapeless pain with color.

She learns to read and write in Spanish by attending night school. It's still difficult for her, although there are situations or words that she's beginning to recognize. She listens to the stories on the radio when she returns from the factory. She irons and prepares meals. Those melodious voices that tell stories of people like her bring her closer to those who work and struggle to survive.

She's been living in this house for quite some time now and she thinks that with a little more in savings she'll be able to rent a room on her own somewhere close to the family. Sarita and José agree with everything she says and does, because she says very little. They'd like her to get out of the house, and accompany them every other week when folks from the old country gather for an evening of socializing.

It was at one of those meetings that she finally went to after giving into her nephews' insistence that she met Pinie, a quiet young man much like her, who enjoys reading like her, and who works in a factory like her.

Since meeting they attend some of the Saturday night socials together. On Sundays they go to the coast for a picnic. He says the city air suffocates him. Pinie loves the river because in Europe he lived in a town that had one running through it.

They don't talk a lot, but they like to eat pastrami sandwiches and pickles that Tinkeleh carries in a net bag with Orange Crush and ice. Being near the river makes them both feel nostalgic. It reminds him of his home town and her of the voyage here on the ship. They buy roasted peanuts and tell each other their family histories, or talk about the characters in the books he reads, or he explains to her in detail different chess moves that are published in the *Di Presse* newspaper.

She listens to him attentively, although she doesn't understand that game that she saw Professor Liebschtein play so often in Terezin. She's startled by the mere memory of a name. However, something keeps her from delving further, even though doing so might be the key to recovering her ability to draw.

She's not in love with Pinie. He arouses tenderness, support, and affection in her. His company pleases her and brings her peace. One afternoon, Pinie shyly takes her hand and kisses her on the mouth, almost carelessly.

36

Today they finally take me to a kind of office where Felipe and Esther are waiting.

They signal to me that I shouldn't talk. They work among the metal filing cabinets with files spread out on desktops.

The place is practically sealed off, but daylight filters in through a small window and hurts my aching eyes.

They kindly explain to me what my job consists of. I don't fully understand what's going on. I can't quite decipher the looks that are exchanged between Esther and the officer seated behind the big desk, nor do I care to. Felipe's signals insist that I keep quiet.

For several hours I type dossiers with names, birth dates, ages, and location of detention. I still can't make sense of what it is I'm doing, but I copy hundreds of names and make note of strange places. Where are the people who belong to these names? I feel like I'm being watched and my discomfort increases with the complicit stares of Esther and Felipe.

They increase the food ration and clean the floor of my cell. The simple gesture puts me in a good mood.

I'm ill at ease digging through the files that pass through my hands over the past several days. I don't want to know about the secret conversations that Esther and the officer are having. Above all Felipe, who mutters between his teeth as he passes by me: "Try to remember every detail, in case you get out." Above all, the longing I feel for Ernesto, the memory of when they took us, the cries of his voice that I heard for two days and nights before they fell silent.

Above all, not being able to see my dreams fulfilled. Above all else, I want to live.

I never derived pleasure from killing, not even the enemy. In fact, I was sickened by those who bragged about it.

I, Rita, daughter of Tinkeleh, granddaughter of Hannah and Rivka, could not think of it without trembling. "What you're saying is suicide," they told me angrily. It's useless to try to make them understand that for me the risk lies elsewhere.

I don't have time to begin the book I wanted to write. I've only got a few lines scribbled on bar napkins. Lines and reflections written in the black oilskin notebook. Political activists can't carry records of any sort, not even of their thoughts. Everything is ephemeral, unattainable. I'm surprised by the optimism of the others, who insist on talking about tomorrow. The past and the present come together in General Perón, in Eva, in the struggle between good and evil, like in the Western cowboy movies that they hate so much. Although they're a lot alike.

I love the cinema as much as I do literature. It's a vice I inherited from my father and even when the risk was high I'd go to the Lorraine movie house and enjoy a good flick.

When the comrades were annoying me with their obsessive criticism I no longer resorted to listening to National Radio, nor playing classical music in a deafening volume. I intensified my risk and took unthinkable actions as a way of challenging them. I'd blast their Glostora Tango Club music.

My mother suspects what I'm up to and she's exasperated by it. She sees the ghosts of her own past made flesh in my attitude. I never told her, and it would have been impossible for her to understand, that it was because of her fading away that I needed to change the world. Our world. Our country. Our America.

I spend several hours a day in this place, this clandestine office.

Each date I copy down, each name I file, each condescending glare from a captor makes me feel that this is a trip to the edge of the abyss. I stretch my body across the void. I see a lot, I hear too much, I file and file, thousands of voices, ages, hair colors, professions, addresses: Auschwitz in Buenos Aires.

These women console me. They know as well as I do where this train is headed. Did I get off at the wrong station? I have no regrets. Yes, I'd like to go home, hop into bed with Ernesto for an afternoon nap, tell Elena and Haydée that we should go back to the bridge over San Martín Avenue and to the Politeama. I want to write it down, all the things I've learned to recognize during my imprisonment and other things that I long to examine straight on. I can't change the world, but I join Eva who departed at 8:25 one winter such as this one.

37

Buenos Aires, January 1948.

She's been married for several months. She no longer works from sunup to sundown or goes to social gatherings on the weekend where everyone speaks at once and no one is particularly bothered by what's happening to others. Living with her cousins and their sons returned her to the real world and helped her to step back and remember who she was then and find out who she is now. Thanks to them she was able to move into a place of her own. She met Pinie, went to night school, and transformed herself from Tinkeleh into Teresa.

Because of them she was able to erase some of her drawings that no longer expressed the same meaning as before. The intensity of those penciled lines had remained behind in Terezin.

How could she explain that she was happy in that nightmarish world? That her most intimate friendships developed in front of a mirror of humiliation and starvation?

How could she come to terms with the fact that sometimes beauty is nourished in horror? It took years for her to uncover those feelings and not be ashamed by them.

She believes that the most difficult part of having to bear survival is the responsibility to complete tasks that others couldn't. But the worst is realizing that what disappeared with the train

that took them from Minsk to Terezin and from Terezin to Auschwitz is irrecoverable. Her drawing hand and her imagination
remain in the boxcar of that last train surrounded by odors that
the passage of time is erasing. Her father's voice, her mother's
face, the chirping of the birds in the woods, the streets of Minsk,
the stones of Terezin were vanishing, but the stench of Auschwitz
still saturates her senses. It's as indelible as the number tattooed
on her wrist.

Among all that chaos Pinie is a soothing balm. She likes that
he's calm and quiet. He works as much as he needs to pay the
rent on the room on Humboldt Street, where they moved after
getting married. Tinkeleh waits for him there with stews she
learned to make at Sarita's house, although hers come out less
oily and she adds more ingredients: meat, potatoes, peas, beans,
corn, and all sorts of vegetables that Pinie really likes. Pinie
tells her admiringly that she cooks very well. She goes to a lot of
trouble to please him.

She doesn't feel the kind of passion for him that Anna Kareni-
na felt for Vronsky, or even that adolescent rush that she'd felt for
Menachem. Menachem . . . Tinkeleh remembers the day she was
in high spirits over the warm bread she was toting home and she
ran into to him. They embraced without saying a word, her small
breasts pressing against the heart pounding inside his chest.

Menachem taught her that it's exciting and dangerous to re-
linquish control of one's body. She can manage her emotions, and
she learned to control her body as well.

She's able to enjoy daily activities with Pinie. She demands almost nothing from him, and he in turn doesn't ask for more than
she seems willing to share.

One Sunday a month they take the subway to the Mundial Cinema downtown. It's a bargain cinema where they show only newsreels from Argentina and around the world. He loves the news and for her, who still understands very little Spanish, the images help with learning the language. After the cinema lets out they go the Pizzeria Las Cuartetas, take a seat at a small, white marble-topped table with discolored golden metal chairs and order a portion of vegetable pizza and a draft beer. They both love the liquor-soaked English pudding for dessert. It reminds her of Hannah's *leikach*. In truth, more than the dessert itself it's the wine they add to it that reminds her of that flavor.

Pizza, beer, and the cinema are things that Pinie introduced to her and now they've become a necessary habit, like the *yerba mate* that she drinks every morning. She started drinking it almost as a game to imitate the other workers at the factory and now it's a daily routine. *Mate* is an inseparable companion. Every neighbor lady on Humboldt has her own unique companion since the *mate* cup comes in all different shapes and sizes, made from different materials, as are the straws used to sip it, which she and the other Jewish women call "*bombilles.*" She knows that it's really pronounced *bombilla*, but she gets a kick out of saying it the other way.

Around this time she talked to Pinie about the need to get a different job because if they were thinking of having children they weren't going to be able to stay in that small space and what they earn isn't enough to rent a larger two-room place. He agrees but it doesn't occur to him to leave the factory and take on a higher paying job like several of the neighbors did who no longer live there. It's clear to Tinkeleh that Pinie is not only unambitious but that he is not willing to make any change toward progress that involves effort. What was up until now a virtue in her marriage is becoming a disappointment.

She's going to have to face the future, though she knows that nothing the future holds is going to be easy. She wants to have a child and that gives her an energy she thought was lost and had all but given up on.

38

Buenos Aires, May 1948.

Pinie is out of sorts, almost unrecognizable.

He's been sleeping poorly for several nights, talking in his sleep and waking up in a cold sweat. She's never seen him in such a state. He turned the radio on early this morning and decided he wasn't going to work.

Several coworkers from the factory arranged to meet at the house.

There's still a little of the whiskey that Pinie has a swig of every afternoon when he gets home from work. He asks that she serve it in several glasses. He's very excited.

It's a cool brisk autumn in Buenos Aires on a pleasant morning with the sun shining at an angle that only happens in the fall.

He takes out two photographs that he purchased at a business in the Once neighborhood. On one it reads "Chaim Weitzman, the first president of Israel," and on the other "Theodor Herzl."

Pinie is euphoric and can scarcely contain himself. His hidden passion reminds Tinkeleh of her classes with Professor Liebschtein in Terezin. Zionism formed a part of her story. Its ideals were defended by some and attacked by others with the limited humility of adolescents in Minsk, where Zionists and the Orthodox became entangled in heated discussions in town, discussions that would be repeated later, in Terezin.

The viability of a Jewish state formed part of those discussions that were cut short, but it was also a space for dreams that some carried forth like a battle standard, a meeting place for those who could think in terms of before and after the death camps.

Zionism, for Pinie, became his primary reason for living. For lack of interest on her part it's not a topic he discusses with her, although seeing him bristling with such enthusiasm moves her.

Friends begin arriving just at the moment in which the United Nations vote is being announced. They jubilantly shout for joy, and the tears they all shed produce in Tinkeleh a newly found sense of emotion, that in recent years has been easier to begin to feel.

Pinie goes to the dark chest of drawers and takes out a shiny silk tallit. He puts on his hat, opens the prayer book, and in a voice rough with emotion intones: *"Baruch Atah Adonai Eloheinu Adonai Echad."*

He is not observant but that gesture in such a measured man fills her with a feeling of tenderness and emotion more moving than the news itself regarding the creation of the State of Israel.

That night she tells him that they are going to have a baby.

39

Felipe and Esther are happier every day and it causes me to distrust them. I try to pretend that all is well while memorizing names and arrest and transfer dates but sometimes I can't bear it. I've been acting like a survivor instead of working as a political activist. The hood over my head forced me for a long while to look only within myself, to delve the depths of a history that I learned anew rather than through friends who observe the world as if it were a household chore. Here, over time, I have been able to value things that before seemed insignificant, like eating, sleeping, working, singing.

Sometimes I dream that I'm sewing yellow stars. Other nights I awake in a cold sweat with the sensation that a piece of the ceiling falls on me and tattoos a burning cross on my skin that peels away like the paint on the wall of my childhood bedroom.

Everything is a puzzle that I try to fit together in brief flashes with the pieces of Tinkeleh's disconnected stories that run contrary to my activism. That idiot Manolo used to say, "The only writing that's worth anything is writing that supports the revolution." His oversimplification of things doesn't manage to hide the fact that when you get right down to it he's a fascist. He is or he was?

I need to maintain my convictions, though every day it becomes harder and harder. I can sense Ernesto at night, his thick lips against my dry abraded skin from which these animals tried to erase any vestige of pleasure.

I jot down a few phrases, random names, numbers.

It is my own Little Larousse dictionary without the illustrations.

Buenos Aires, November 1948.

When Tinkeleh awakens following the caesarean, it all comes together. There she is, with the feeling of being on a path that she's forced to follow in order to reclaim her history through her daughter.

In Yiddish she'll be called Rivka, after her grandmother. In the language of this country where she was reborn and which is beginning to feel like her own, she'll be Rita, like the Santa Rita, the beautiful flower that grows in front of her house on Humboldt Street. Although, rather than being a saint she hopes she'll be a Rita as strong and sensitive as her grandmother, in a long family line that finds continuity through her.

Given the comments I overheard from some of the guards, I don't just sense it, I know it.

The files are almost finished, but we try to drag the work out because we suspect that our stay here depends on it.

I'm hearing the word "transfer" too frequently over the past few days.

"Transfer" sounds like transport to me. Transfers and transports are done in train cars or perhaps something more modern. Automobile? Airplane? Boat?

I scribble on the wall: "*Arbeit Macht Frei.*" Is it just a sentence or is it a sentence? I then add "Rita" to my collection of women, the showcase-gynaeceum that accompanies me wherever I go.

The sun is so intense that it seems to illuminate everything, spilling through that little window in the office where we work. It's like a stranger trying to invade the dark intimacy among the small gestures of my life.

I recall a verse by Borges that I read a long time ago: "In war, I am an echo, oblivion, nothing."

Am I an echo, oblivion, nothing? I ask, flooded in the strange light.

The fat man enters with his head down and says to me: "You're being transferred tomorrow."

The stories of rabbis are based on *Tales of the Hasidim* by Martin Buber.

Chapter 25 is based on the book *The Terezin Requiem* by Josef Bor.

The poems by Miroslav Kosek and Franta Bass appear in the book *Children's Drawings and Poems, Terezín, 1942–1944*.

About the Author and Translator

Argentine author **Manuela Fingueret** is a storyteller, poet, journalist, essayist, and editor. She lives in Buenos Aires. www.manuelafingueret.com.ar

Darrell B. Lockhart is chair of the departments of Spanish and Portuguese at the University of Nevada, Reno.